KILL OR BE KILLED

Kill or Be Killed

A Patrick Dawlish Mystery

John Creasey *writing as* Gordon Ashe

OPEN ROAD
INTEGRATED MEDIA
NEW YORK

ISBN: 978-1-5040-9811-3

This edition published in 2024 by Open Road Integrated Media, Inc.
180 Maiden Lane
New York, NY 10038
www.openroadmedia.com

KILL OR BE KILLED

CHAPTER I

THE BODY BY THE GATE

The gate creaked open, and the man leaned against it, gasping for breath. Ahead, friendly lights shone from two downstairs windows of the house. The curtains weren't drawn. The man saw a woman, with her back to him, and heard the faint strains of music from radio or gramophone. He gripped the top of the gate tightly and stood erect, holding his breath. His eyes glistened when they caught the light, were dull when he turned to look along the road.

He saw no one—only the shadowy shapes of trees and bushes, the lighted windows of another house which was much farther away, and the headlamps of a car on a distant road, casting a pale white glow. He saw no other movement, heard no other sound.

He let go of the gate and stepped unsteadily towards the house.

The drive was steep. There were high banks on either side, topped by trees and shrubs. Wind rustled the autumn leaves as if with whispering menace; the man stopped, not two yards from the gate, and peered to his right.

Was someone moving?

Or was it a bush, bending in the breeze? It was just a bush, and—

He heard a sound behind him, whirled in terror, and opened his mouth. But the dark figure, springing from the left bank, was on him before he could shout. A knife glittered, and pain streaked through his chest as the blade struck home. A hand smothered his mouth and bent him backwards; the knife gave a queer, sucking sound as it was withdrawn; a duller one as it was driven in again.

The victim's legs crumpled, and he fell.

The murderer bent over him, pulled out the knife, went down on one knee and peered at him closely; there was no doubt that he was dead.

The murderer stood up, turned and wiped the blade on the grass of the bank, then pushed it in and out of the soil to clean it thoroughly. Next, he put the knife into his breast pocket, and bent over his victim again. For the first time, he looked at the house. The sound of music continued to float gently towards him as he started to feel inside the dead man's pockets, one after the other. His hair stirred in another gentle gust of wind.

Before his task was finished, he heard footsteps—

Patrick Dawlish looked at his wife as she knitted, read a story in a shiny magazine, and appeared, in spite of all this, to listen to the concerto which the Third Programme was offering its listeners. His Felicity was not beautiful; but her face held warmth and calmness, her lips were full and generous, and for him she had beauty.

On a small table by his side a tankard of beer stood next to a book, lying open face downwards, and an ashtray. A large pipe drooped from his lips. In the days of his youth, a well-directed punch had broken his nose. That was a good thing, for it spoiled perfection of feature and gave him a homely look.

He smoothed down his corn-coloured hair, still staring at his wife.

She turned over a page; the music rose to a climax with an overtone of drums. Felicity looked up, not at him, but at the radio, which fitted neatly into a carved cupboard. A modern radio in that period room would have looked incongruous.

The concerto came to an end; the applause began slowly.

Felicity stretched out her hand and switched off the radio, let the knitting fall into her lap and the magazine to the floor. 'I've noticed it for the last few days. You haven't concentrated on anything, but mooned about all day as if you were a caged beast.'

'We've finished picking the apples, and there isn't much to do on the farm,' said Dawlish. 'My mind roams. How about a few days on the Continent? Anywhere but Monte Carlo would suit me. Or even a few days in London? Theatres and things. Man needs relaxation after his toil, and—'

'We're going to Town next week. You told me so.'

'Well, well!' murmured Dawlish. 'So we are, and I'd forgotten.' He got up and stretched, and the tips of his fingers touched the ceiling, for he stood six-foot-three and weighed more than fifteen stone.

'You can't settle to the radio, or a book, or me, or anything,' declared Felicity, and looked at him with a thoughtful, almost accusing eye. 'Is anything up? Has Trivett—'

'Hold it. I've almost forgotten there is a policeman named Trivett.' Dawlish chuckled, and rested a hand lightly on her hair. 'No funny business, my poppet. I hold no secrets from you. Crime does not beckon, and—'

'It does,' said Felicity. 'Whether you like it and whether I like it, it always will, I suppose. Sometimes I wish you'd never won that diabolic reputation of yours. Then I remember that if you hadn't we probably shouldn't have met.'

'Confusing,' agreed Dawlish. 'Darling, all I want is a bit of a break. Not Dawlish the Dude Detective, just a change of scene but not of company. How about Paris after London?'

'I'd love it,' said Felicity.

'Fine! And how about a spot of night air right now?'

'I don't feel like going out to-night,' said Felicity. 'It's a bit cold outside. I'll go up, I think, and read in bed for a bit.'

'I won't be long,' promised Dawlish.

When he had gone, Felicity leaned back in her chair and closed her eyes. Pat might not realise it himself, but he was restless. He was a natural detective. Problems intrigued him, crime fascinated him, mystery brought out in him qualities which anyone knowing him casually would not suspect were there. If his friend Trivett of Scotland Yard were to ring up now and say: 'Fel, I've got a job for Pat,' she'd be glad. Unless it really happened, of course, when she'd hate it and fight against it, but have to suffer all the consequences.

Dawlish sauntered along, filling his pipe, enjoying the crisp night air. He was half-way down the drive when he heard a sound.

Night noises were familiar: he could tell the carefree scuttle of a rabbit from the stealthy creeping of a fox, the soft rustle of a bird disturbed, the swift sudden swoop of a bat. All were friendly noises to him. That sound had not been friendly. A man had made it furtively.

He couldn't see the gate, for it was oiled dark brown, but he could make out the shapes of trees against a cloudy sky. He saw something move—another dark shape which reached the top of the left-hand bank, then disappeared. It was a man, his footsteps muffled by the grass; Dawlish had heard them on the gravel of the drive.

A burglar?

He was up to no good, or he wouldn't have scuttled off like that. He was probably heading for a stile which led from Dawlish's grounds to a meadow; and the meadow was bordered by a by-road.

Dawlish moved swiftly up the steep bank and across the tree-studded grassland. He knew the quickest way to the road well.

He did not see his quarry again until he was ten yards from the stile.

The man was climbing over it.

Dawlish followed, and saw him making a bee-line for the gate which led to the road.

Dawlish didn't climb the stile, but turned towards the road itself, and went along on the inside of the hedge. Here the grass was short and the ground even; he ran, until he reached the road-hedge, and peered over.

Two things showed against the pale surface of the road.

One, near, was a woman, walking towards him. She was on the grass verge, or he would have heard her before.

The other was a car, parked at the side of the road.

Dawlish waited until the woman had passed him, then he squeezed through the hedge and hurried towards the car. As he drew near, his quarry appeared from the meadow, and a man called from the car:

'Okay?'

'Someone's about—step on it.'

The door opened, not ten yards away from Dawlish. He covered the ground as the engine whined before breaking into a steady hum. The man who climbed in slammed the door—and as soon as it closed, Dawlish pulled it open.

'What the—'

'Not so fast,' said Dawlish, stretching out his hand. 'I want a word with you, son.'

He clapped his great hands on the man's shoulder, felt the fellow wriggle—but didn't see the other's right hand move towards his pocket. The driver didn't speak, but let in the clutch; the car began to move. Dawlish held on, intending to drag the man out of his seat; then the knife flashed and red-hot pain struck the back of his left hand. He winced and let go. The car shot away, the door slammed again, and blood welled up from the gash in Dawlish's hand.

CHAPTER II

THE GIRL BY THE BODY

The car swung round a corner, to the right. There was only one road from there, running through Haslemere. A call to the local police should be in time to have the road blocked. Dawlish turned and hurried towards his gate, pulling out his handkerchief, wadding it and pressing it on to the wound. He drew within a few yards of his gate. Felicity hadn't gone upstairs yet; the sitting-room light still blazed.

A wild, ear-splitting scream came from the drive, just out of his sight. It made him jump. A second scream ended in a gasping, sobbing note, and before it faded, Dawlish was at the gateway. He could just discern a girl standing over the body which lay there; and as he watched, she crumpled up and fell across the body.

The front door opened and Felicity appeared, a silhouette against the light. Dawlish shouted:

'Fel—can you hear me?'

'Yes!' came clearly.

'Telephone the police. Small car, ten horse-power, dark saloon, Haslemere road—must be stopped.'

Felicity was already turning round.

Dawlish felt his hand throbbing, touched the handkerchief and found it soaked with blood. He bound it tightly round his wrist, and bent his elbow, as if his arm were in a sling. He went down on one knee and eased the girl off the man; she was a dead weight, but only unconscious. He set her against the bank. Her head lolled forward. On her pale face there was a dark smear.

He bent over the man.

He didn't need much light to see that murder had been done.

As he straightened up, the throbbing of his hand grew much worse.

Far off, the headlights of a car—probably *the* car—showed on the Haslemere road. Inside the house, Felicity was calling the police.

Felicity came hurrying down the drive, with Hilda, their maid and general factotum, by her side. Dawlish leaned against the bank, looking down at the unconscious girl. Felicity called: 'Are you all right, Pat?' and Dawlish answered: 'Yes. Hilda, go back to the house, telephone the police, and ask them to send detectives and a doctor here, at once. Say that it's serious.'

She turned and stumbled up the drive, while Felicity came towards Dawlish. 'What is it, Pat?'

'Murder,' he said bluntly. 'We've a fainting girl on our hands, too. Not to mention a slightly wounded husbands—but it's only a scratch. Hallo, she's coming round.'

Felicity reached them as the girl suddenly drew in her breath, then began to moan: '*No, no, no, no!*'

'Get her up to the house,' said Dawlish. 'She'll be all right.'

He moved abruptly, leaving the two women, and strode up the drive, going to one side of the house. The garage at the back was locked; and the keys were in his left trouser pocket; he had to use his injured hand; a painful business, but he got the keys.

He switched the garage light on, and took a flashlamp which hung on a nail in the wall, and a wash-leather gardening glove from the bench, then hurried back to the drive. Felicity was half-way up, with her arm round the girl.

Near the dead man, he shone the torch. Blood had soaked the man's shirt and dribbled on to the drive. The pale face was that of a young man, and not bad-looking. The coat was open, and one side was flat against the ground. Dawlish put the glove on and felt inside the pocket. It was empty.

He went through all the other pockets he could get at without shifting the body, and found a cigarette-case, a lighter, a penknife, two latch-keys, and some loose change; that was all. He put all the things back, then turned the body over gently, exerting himself not to let the corpse fall on its face, and felt for the hip pocket.

He drew out a bunch of keys.

There was something else: a small note-book. He dropped keys and note-book into his own pocket before arranging the body again just as he had found it.

His left hand seemed to be on fire.

He shone the flashlight on to it.

The gash looked deep but clean. The edges were puffy and discoloured with blood, but most of the bleeding had stopped; the handkerchief bound tightly round his wrist caused most of the pain. He loosened it, and after a moment the throbbing eased.

He took out the note-book, tucked the flashlight under his arm, and looked through the pages. The book was about three inches by two, and felt stiff and new. There were several addresses; what looked like a shopping list; half a dozen telephone numbers. He found it difficult to turn each page with the glove on, but didn't use his bare fingers.

The last note was on the end page, and he bent closer, so as to read: *Dawlish, Fourways, Alum, Nr. Hindhead.*

He closed the book and put it inside the dead man's breast pocket. That done, he glanced towards the road and saw the headlights of a car, some distance off, but heading this way.

It was one o'clock.

The body had been photographed by flashlight and taken into Haslemere. Police were still searching the grounds for clues—footprints, any odd things.

The girl was in the spare room, sleeping. The police-surgeon had allowed the police to question her a little, and then had given her veronal, to help her to rest and recover from the shock. She had told them that she had arranged to meet her fiancé at this house, but swore she didn't know why. Dawlish remembered how she had twisted the new engagement ring round and round on her finger as she talked.

Her fiancé's name was Ryan—Mick Ryan. Hers was Helen Graves.

Hilda was in bed, but almost certainly awake. Dawlish, his hand heavily bandaged and throbbing only a little, sat in the winged arm-chair, with a tankard of beer by his side, the book still open face downwards on the table, and the pipe drooping from his lips.

Felicity, without her knitting or the magazine, sat on a footstool and stared gravely up at him.

'I wish you wouldn't lie to me,' she said in a flat voice. 'I'd much rather know what you're up to. You always have your own way, so why try to keep it a secret from me? You've known something was going to happen. You knew that boy, and probably know the girl. You've been on edge, waiting for this to blow up.'

'It was as much a surprise to me as it was to you.'

'I don't believe it.'

So, constraint fell upon them.

It lasted for some time, even while Felicity helped Dawlish to undress, for his hand was stiff and heavily bandaged. He had been engaged in counter-espionage work; since then he had occasionally been asked to assist the police, and several times had become involved 'by accident.' In fact, there were occasions when he felt so restless that he went out to look for trouble.

'Awake, Fel?' he asked.

'Yes. I thought you—Pat, didn't you know anything about it?'

'It's hard to believe that a man was killed on the drive, without my knowing, but he was. Almost as hard to believe I got my hands on his killer and let him go, but I did.'

Silence followed, and with it an easing of the constraint, although neither moved nor spoke. Then slowly her arm crept across his chest, and she edged nearer.

'Sorry, Pat.'

Later, when he lay drowsing, he thought lazily about many things, but most of all about the bunch of keys which lay in the drawer of the bedside table. He *ought* to hand them over to the police. . . .

When he woke again the birds were greeting the dawn noisily, Felicity was sleeping soundly. He heard nothing that might have awakened him, and looked at the door.

It was opening!

He watched through his lashes.

The movement was slow and stealthy. He eased himself over to one side, so that he could spring out of bed quickly.

Then he saw a hand at the door; a slim, white hand.

The girl peered in.

Her dark hair was attractively tousled, her eyes heavy after the drugged sleep. She was fully dressed.

She stepped into the room, watching him and Felicity intently. She didn't close the door, but took two or three hesitant steps towards the bed, then turned to the dressing-table. Nothing there interested her. She stepped to his clothes, which were folded over a chair at the foot of the bed, and kept darting swift, nervous glances at him as she went through the pockets, looking for—what?

She was of medium height, and her clothes fitted her well, although a little too tightly for her figure. A button of her white blouse was undone. She bit her lips as if in vexation, went to the dressing-table and pulled open the top drawer. Oddments of combs, brushes, and make-up clinked and rattled a little, and she caught her breath.

Felicity wasn't disturbed.

The girl finished at the dressing-table, turned and stared at Dawlish—and he was afraid that she knew that he was awake.

She stepped towards the head of the bed, keyed-up, forcing herself to keep on with the search.

She opened the drawer of the bedside table; the keys jingled.

He heard her sharp intake of breath. The temptation to look at her was almost irresistible, but he didn't move his head. She took the keys out, held them just in his sight, then lifted them up, as if to gloat over them.

Then she turned and went swiftly to the door.

CHAPTER III

THE KEYS AND THE GIRL

The girl cast a final, frightened and furtive glance behind her, and the door closed. Felicity stirred. Dawlish got out of bed and reached for his dressing-gown.

'What time is it?' asked Felicity sleepily.

'Early. I won't be long,' whispered Dawlish.

When he reached the landing, all the doors were closed. He looked over the banisters and saw her dark head below him. He sped down after her, making little sound.

She fumbled with the bolts and chain as he went into the morning-room.

He opened a window, climbed on to a flower-bed, turned towards the porch. He saw a policeman's helmet near the gate.

He stood by the porch as the front door opened and the girl came out. She didn't close the door behind her—and didn't see him until she reached the three porch steps. Then he moved forward, gigantic and frightening, and she uttered a little cry and shrank away.

Dawlish beamed. 'Why, good morning!'

She didn't answer.

He took her arm, and felt her shivering. 'Couldn't you rest? How about a cup of tea?'

Still she didn't answer.

She was young: in the early twenties. She had a strong face, with a good chin, and her eyes were dark brown. The top of her head didn't come up to his shoulder.

'No, I—I couldn't sleep,' she said, in a quivering voice. 'I seem to see him all the time, with the blood—'

Dawlish put a hand on her shoulder.

'Yes, I know. Bad. But people will help, you know.' He led her into the hall, then along the kitchen passage. The hands of the frying-pan clock, over the high mantelshelf, pointed to five minutes past six. Dawlish filled an electric kettle and switched on. The girl stood near the door, still frightened, one hand at her breast, as if to protect the keys.

'Why—why did they *do* it?' she asked helplessly.

'The police will find out.'

'The *police*!' Scorn put strength into her voice. 'If the police were any good, Mick wouldn't be—'

She stopped.

Dawlish missed the obvious opening, shook his head sadly, and said: 'Sit down. I'll get some biscuits.' He went into the larder.

It was more than a larder, really a large storeroom with another door which led to the kitchen passage. He snatched a tin from the shelf, took off the lid and dropped it with a clatter, then went into the passage and turned to the back door. He reached the door a second in front of the girl; and again she came upon his vast figure when she thought she was safe.

This time Dawlish spoke sharply.

'Even if you were to get into the grounds, the police would probably stop you. If they let you go, they'd follow you. And they'd want to know, sooner or later, why you ran away.'

'Damn the police!'

'That isn't so easy. If you run away now, they may think you know something about it. The name of the killer, for instance.'

'I don't!'

'But you know a great deal that you haven't told them. What's it all about, Helen?'

'Nothing! You've no right to keep me here.' She dived to one side thrusting at him, and tried to pass. He grabbed her round the waist and lifted her off her feet.

'Let me go!' She kicked and struggled. 'Let me go, I've a right to go!'

'Later,' said Dawlish.

Using his left hand was no fun; but he used it, holding her by the waist and, before she realised what was happening, turning her upside down.

The keys clinked on the floor.

'Up-sa-daisy,' murmured Dawlish. He turned her upright and stood her on her feet. She reeled back against the wall, her cheeks flaming red. Her skirt was rucked up near her waist, and Dawlish stretched out a hand to pull the skirt down when Felicity said:

'Very pretty. Shall I do that?'

The girl gasped for breath as Felicity straightened her clothes and pushed her hair back from her face. Her brown eyes were stormy with anger and vexation.

The keys were at Dawlish's feet.

Then the girl flew at him, striking his face and kicking at his shins, making him draw back. She bent down swiftly and snatched at the keys, but before she touched them, Dawlish's massive foot covered them. She drew back, shouting shrilly in hysterical rage, and kicked again. Felicity caught her arm, dragged her away from Dawlish and slapped her face sharply.

She pulled herself free from Felicity and leapt at Dawlish again. Felicity took her by the hair, pulled her round, and gave her a second slap. This time Felicity was angry.

There was a moment of strange, strained tension; then Helen buried her face in her hands and began to cry. Felicity's expression softened. She put her arm round the girl's shoulder, and said:

'I'll look after her.'

'Don't be too gentle,' said Dawlish, rubbing his face gingerly. He stooped down for the keys and dropped them into his pocket, wishing that his hand would stop throbbing. 'These caused the trouble. She pinched 'em and tried to make off. I'm not sure that she's really hysterical. She can put on a good act.'

'This isn't an act,' said Felicity, and led the girl into the kitchen.

Dawlish shrugged his shoulders, opened the back door, and looked into the grounds. No police were near; apparently they'd heard nothing. He took out the keys and inspected them carefully. Several were ordinary Yale keys, indistinguishable one from the other, but four were from a Chaldon safe. Chaldon safes were very good and extremely expensive, and there weren't many about. He wrapped the keys in his handkerchief and went back to the kitchen.

Helen sat in an easy-chair, her head resting against the back, her eyes closed; the spots of colour had faded into pasty pallor. She looked ill and spent. Felicity poured boiling water into the tea-pot. The large kitchen, with its shiny white tiles, caught the early sun, and was bright and cheerful.

Helen's hand was unsteady when she took the cup and saucer, but she managed to sip and then to drink. Dawlish sat on a corner of the table while he drank his tea, and felt the weight of the keys resting against his side. No one else stirred, inside or outside; but Hilda would be up at about seven; it was now twenty-five minutes to.

Dawlish said: 'Why do you want the keys, Helen? Tell me or tell the police. No other choice. If your reason's strong enough, I'll keep your secret. If it isn't—'

'They're not yours, you've no right to them,' she muttered. 'You ought to give them to me.'

'I've told you what I'll do,' said Dawlish. There were times, like this, when he could manage better without Felicity; if he got really tough, the girl would break down and tell him everything.

'What's it to be—the police or me?'

'It—it doesn't make any difference,' she mumbled.

'Mick Ryan thought it would,' said Dawlish.

Her eyes blazed. 'How do you know?' She glared at him, almost accusingly; and the glint which sprang to Felicity's eyes suggested that she read his words as an admission that he'd known about Mick Ryan before.

'*How do you know?*' Helen screeched.

Dawlish said: 'Mick had a new note-book. There were several names and addresses in it—one of them was mine. He was in trouble, and thought I could help him out, that's why he came here last night. Why did *you* come, Helen?'

'I've told you. I was to meet—'

'That's what you told the police. I want the truth.'

She evaded his eyes.

Felicity flashed Dawlish a message; part apology, part encouragement: 'Handle it your way, Pat.' Dawlish leaned forward and tapped the girl's knee.

'Why did you come? Just to get the keys?'

'I—no!'

'Then why?'

She started to speak, but couldn't finish; tears flooded her eyes again. She sat back as if tormented; the tears trickled down her cheek. She looked hopeless and helpless, in a distress which should have melted most hard hearts.

Dawlish said coldly: 'Fel, go for the policeman at the gates.'

Felicity promptly moved towards the door.

Helen opened her eyes. She darted an appealing glance at Felicity, who stood by the door, quite unmoved. Dawlish took out the handkerchief, unfolded it, and tossed the keys gently up and down.

'Either you tell me everything, or I send for the police and hand these over,' he said.

She didn't answer.

'All right,' said Dawlish crisply. 'Call that policeman, Fel.'

Helen gasped: 'No! No, I'll tell you!'

CHAPTER IV

THE GIRL TELLS A STORY

'It's been going on for months,' said Helen.

'What has?' asked Felicity.

'All—this.' Helen waved her hands. 'It wasn't long after I met Mick. And—and fell in love with him.' Tears welled up in her eyes again, and her voice broke. 'I can't believe—he's dead. I'm sorry I've behaved terribly. It's been such a strain. Mick—Mick worked for Lord Calder—Jeremiah Calder. You know him, don't you?'

Dawlish shot a warning glance at Felicity, and schooled his voice to sound casual.

'The great and mysterious Jeremiah, with a finger in many pies, and a keen dislike of publicity. Yes, I've heard of him.'

'He trusted Mick. Mick worked for him for years. When we met, Mick—Mick was thoroughly happy. He'd a job for life, a good job, everything he could want. And then something happened to Jeremiah Calder. It wasn't long after he was made a baron. It puzzled Mick. Jeremiah stopped being friendly. He didn't trust anyone, except Mick. He employed two men—body-guards, Mick called them. He behaved as if he were frightened out of his wits. He wouldn't go anywhere alone, seldom left his house. He and Mick used to travel about a lot, but all that stopped. Mick asked him what it was, and Jeremiah snapped his head off. Mick grew more and more worried, because it was making Jeremiah ill. Sometimes he was confined to his room for days on end. Mick knew there was something serious the matter, of course, and—and he tried to find out what it was. He noticed a man hanging about outside the house. Mick lived in Lord Calder's house, you see—it was his home. He followed the man. And—he couldn't have done a worse thing. The man led him through the back streets of the East End. Two others came along, and they beat Mick up.'

'How long ago was this?' asked Dawlish.

'About—about three weeks ago. They gave Mick a terrible beating. He was black and blue when he came back. And—they told him he'd get something worse if he didn't do what they wanted. Which was to steal—'

Emotion overcame her again, in a great flood.

'The keys?' murmured Dawlish.

'Y-yes. Those accursed keys!' Helen looked at them as they lay in the white handkerchief. 'These men wanted the keys to the house; and to the strong room and the safe. They gave Mick a week to get them. He didn't try. He—'

'Did he tell Jeremiah Calder about this?'

'No, he—he didn't want to worry his Chief, he just kept it to himself—explained that he'd had an accident. He didn't want to tell me, but I wormed the truth out of him. After the week passed nothing happened for a few days. Then—then they caught Mick again. He was on his way to see me, one night. They stopped him in the street and forced him into a car. They—tortured him.' She broke off, shuddering. 'They said it was nothing to what they'd do if he didn't get those keys. But he didn't—he told the police, although they'd warned him not to. He told the police at Scotland Yard. I made him! He went there after dark one day and told them, and—they didn't do anything. They didn't seem to believe him. Don't talk about the police to me; they—they're rogues. They get a rake-off!'

Dawlish didn't speak.

'And then they started on me,' said Helen.

She shivered again.

'They stopped me in the street, made me get into a car, kept me a prisoner, and—and then told Mick. They said they'd kill me if he didn't get the keys. Mick was frantic, desperate, and he got the keys. He wouldn't give them up until they'd released me. That—that was only yesterday. So they let me go. Mick telephoned last night. About seven o'clock. He told me he wasn't going to give the keys up, he couldn't trust the police, and—he was coming to see you. Someone had given him your name and said you—you would help. I begged him not to, begged him to give the keys up, but he wouldn't. He—he didn't ask me to meet him,' she confessed, and caught her breath again. 'He told me to stay indoors until I heard from him. But I couldn't rest, I had to come and see if he got here safely. I had to come, and then—I found him dead. Murdered. They'd threatened to kill him, and they did it. They—they'll do anything to get those keys!'

'So you were going to hand them over,' said Dawlish.

'Yes!' Suddenly she jumped up. 'Yes, I was! I'm so frightened.'

'What haven't you told me?' asked Dawlish. 'What else happened last night, Helen—between the time you telephoned Mick—'

'He telephoned me.'

'You know what I mean. What else happened?' When she didn't answer, he went on: 'You had a visitor—a call from these people, didn't you?'

'Yes!' she sobbed. 'Yes, I did. They terrified me. If I hadn't told them, they'd have killed me—I know they would. It's my fault he's dead: I'm really the murderer!'

'Did you come here to warn him what you'd done?' asked Dawlish heavily.

'Yes. But who'll believe me? I came to tell him to be careful—I just had to. And then—then I stumbled on his body. I saw what they'd done. And—and they'd told me what they'd do to me. And—I knew Mick had the keys last night. The police didn't find them. So I thought—you might—have found them. I was going to take them away and give them up.'

She groped for the chair, and dropped into it.

Dawlish's voice was like a saw working on hard wood.

'Supposing it's true, up to the moment you found him dead. What was your little game after that? You couldn't save Mick by taking the keys. Where were you going to take them?'

He took her arm and pulled her to her feet; she was helpless, although he was only using his one sound hand. He shook her and pushed her back into the chair. Felicity stretched out a hand, as if in protest, but didn't utter a word.

Helen Graves cowered back from the stern bleakness of Dawlish's face.

'I—I couldn't—help—myself. I was so—frightened. Terrified!'

'Did you come here to try to stop Mick from giving them to me?'

'Yes, that's right. It wasn't any use—fighting. I knew it wasn't. They're too—powerful. Too—powerful. I'm so frightened of them.'

'Where were you going to take them?'

'To—Piccadilly Underground—the subway by Swan and Edgar.'

'When?'

24

'Any time—to-day.'

'You'll be there,' said Dawlish. 'And you'll do what I tell you, my pet, or you'll have more than Mick's ghost to haunt you. Now go up to your room and rest. If you try to get away again, you'll have to deal with the police, not with me.'

She went out, dragging her feet; and Dawlish didn't think there was any need to follow her.

Felicity said: 'What are you going to do now?'

'Have a false set of keys made. Give them to her. Be at Piccadilly when she meets the messenger, and then follow him. A.B.C. Beyond that—' He shrugged his shoulders. 'One jump ahead's not bad for a start.'

'I suppose not,' said Felicity slowly. 'But—there's your hand. And—they're killers. The police—'

'This mob will smell a copper a mile off, but they're not so used to the scent of dude sleuths. I'll enlist Ted and Tim, who're always ready for some fun, and will look after me.' He grinned.

'Supposing Helen tells the police what she's told us?'

Dawlish rested his hand on her shoulders.

'You haven't had enough sleep, darling. She won't. She hasn't told us why she's frightened of the law, but she's far too frightened to talk. Just now, the only way to get results is to side-step the police.'

CHAPTER V

SCARS ON THE BODY

Inspector Allen came into the Dawlish's dining-room, and apologised for interrupting breakfast. He was tall, slim, and neat; a diffident man, but tenacious. How had the girl slept? Had she shown any disposition to talk? Could he see her now?

'Up to the sawbones,' said Dawlish. 'Have you brought him with you?'

'The doctor promised to be here at nine o'clock, and it's ten to now,' said Allen.

'Then have a cup of coffee while you wait. Any helpful hints from the body?'

'I thought you might like to see it.'

'If there's time,' said Dawlish casually. 'I have to run up to town to-day.'

'We'll go to the morgue straight from here, and take the girl with us, if she's well enough,' Allen said. 'Yes, thanks, Mrs. Dawlish, I'd like a cup of coffee.'

'Any arrest?' asked Dawlish mildly.

Allen kept a solemn face. 'Not yet.' He coloured slightly and reproved: 'If your telephone message had come in a minute earlier, we might have caught that car. Odd thing about that car—we had the roads watched, and it wasn't seen. Several small, dark saloons were stopped, but the drivers and passengers all gave good accounts of themselves.'

'Odd is the word,' agreed Dawlish.

'Could the car belong to someone local?'

'Why not? On the other hand, why?' asked Dawlish. 'I don't think there's a local angle. Ryan got my address from someone, and came out here.'

'Someone who knew your reputation,' murmured Allen.

The police-surgeon arrived then, and decreed that Helen Graves, although still in a nervous state, could safely be questioned. After all, Allen took her off first, after arranging to see Dawlish at the police-station an hour later. One policeman remained at the gate, but otherwise *Four Ways* was quite normal. Hilda's tactics were to pretend that nothing untoward had happened. She wore a long-suffering look, but went about her work briskly.

In the drawing-room, Felicity asked Dawlish:

'Where are you going to get the other keys made? In Haslemere?'

'No fear! All the tradesmen are Allen's cronies. In town.'

'I think I'll come to town with you,' said Felicity.

It took Dawlish twenty minutes to persuade her to drop the idea.

Allen's office was small, warm, and crowded. On a little table by the window was a collection of personal oddments, most of them familiar to Dawlish. The latch-keys; the knife; the small change; the little note-book, all from Ryan's pockets. Allen strolled to the table and said:

'You didn't find anything else, did you?'

'Your job, old chap, not mine.'

'You didn't know Ryan or the girl, did you?'

'You're as sceptical as my wife. What about Helen Graves, by the way? Holding her?'

'Her story seems all right, so we're letting her go,' said Allen. 'I'll send her home by car. I've asked Scotland Yard to keep an eye on her. She lives in a small flat in Fulham with her mother, who's a chronic invalid.'

'I'll take her up,' offered Dawlish.

'Oh. Yes, good idea. But I'd like you to have a look at the body first.'

Why was Allen so anxious that he should see Ryan in the morgue?

The morgue attendant got up from a stool where he had been reading a newspaper, and switched on the light.

'Want me, sir?'

'Not yet,' said Allen. He went casually across to a corner table and pulled the top of a sheet back. Dawlish saw Ryan's face for the second time.

Good-looking kid, he thought; with dark, curly hair and full, generous lips. The chin was rather weak; that didn't mean a thing.

Allen drew the sheet farther back.

He watched Dawlish as he did so, a look which Dawlish knew only too well. Allen hoped to see some change of expression indicating that this was an ordeal, because Allen didn't believe his story. Dawlish saw the ugly stab wounds, with ridges where the flesh had been pierced. That wasn't all; on both breasts there were recent burn-scars. In the middle of the flat stomach was another burn mark, larger than a half-crown; although it was partly healed it still looked red and sore.

Allen beckoned the attendant. Between them, they turned the corpse over. 'We've got all the photographs we want,' Allen said, and darted another shrewd look at Dawlish, as if to see how this affected him.

Dawlish clamped his teeth together.

Ryan's back was a criss-cross of ugly weals; wounds barely healed, which had been caused by a cat-o'-nine-tails or a similar weapon. The wounds started between the shoulder blades and finished in the small of the back.

'Expert,' said Dawlish. 'Expert devil. Look for an old salt.'

'I don't understand you.'

'You would, if you'd ever seen a sergeant-at-arms use the cat, before the Navy became civilised and stopped it. They're the only men expert at it, outside the prison service, and I can't see an ex-warder at this job. Does your doctor say how long ago this was done?'

The keys jingled in his pocket as he drew out a handkerchief to wipe his forehead.

Allen said: 'The flogging was done three to four weeks ago. The burns, ten days to a fortnight. Dawlish, are you prepared to go into the witness-box and swear you've never seen this man until last night?'

'I am,' said Dawlish.

He knew that Allen still didn't believe him.

If he hadn't known then, he would have discovered it very soon. He started along the London road with a subdued Helen by his side, and a police-car followed them. He dawdled, deliberately, for the first few miles, and the car made no attempt to overtake him.

Helen didn't speak.

Dawlish opened the throttle a little, and said:

'How much did you tell the police?'

'Nothing.'

Dawlish noticed the quick, scared glance she gave him; she was afraid that he was going to ask more questions. He left her in peace. She closed her eyes, dozed most of the journey. When they were on the outskirts of London, on the Kingston by-pass, Dawlish spoke again.

'Listen carefully. You'll go to your home, stay indoors until five o'clock, and not leave for any reason unless the police send for you. If anyone comes, saying he is a policeman, telephone this number.' He handed her a card. 'Tim Jeremy is a friend of mine. That's his number, and he'll know all about you. Then go straight to Leicester Square, and stand in front of the statue, facing the Odeon Cinema. A man will come up and give you a package; it'll contain keys, but not those I have. Go along to your Piccadilly rendezvous, and hand the keys over to anyone who asks for them. Refuse to go with him, whatever he says. Say you'll scream, say anything—but don't go with him. Understand that?'

'Supposing he forces me to?'

'He can't, at Piccadilly Circus. If there looks like being trouble, kick up a fuss. Don't go with him, and—this is just as important—don't speak to him, except to refuse to leave the spot. Don't say another word. If you do what I tell you, you won't need to worry about the police much longer.'

Dawlish slowed down at Putney, and asked for her address; it was in Fulham, not far from Putney Bridge.

Dawlish thrust open her door, glancing behind him as he did so. The police-car was parked a little farther along. Would it follow him, or Helen? He sat and watched her walk towards her home, a forlorn, dejected figure. She didn't look round. The police-car followed and slowed down; a detective jumped out and went in her wake.

The police-car stayed where it was.

Dawlish drove on to Hammersmith Broadway, where he turned left, towards Chiswick. There he went along narrow streets—a rabbit warren in which any stranger would get lost. He was not a stranger to them. Nor was the driver of the small saloon car which he had noticed for the first time in Wimbledon, and which was still close behind him. The driver wore a bowler hat.

Dawlish called at a small shop to get some cigarettes, then drove off again and was followed to the West End.

CHAPTER VI

TWO SETS OF KEYS

London was thronged with traffic and people. Oxford Street seemed more crowded than usual; the doors of the big stores constantly opened and closed. Policemen stood impassive near the changing traffic lights. Dawlish's Lagonda obeyed them all; so did the small saloon car. Dawlish turned into Regent Street, rounded Piccadilly Circus, where Eros greeted him, and drove down the Haymarket, along Pall Mall and turned into Waterloo Place. He slowed down, as if to admire the spacious greenery of St. James's Park. Then he turned right, and soon reached the entrance to his club.

His club was large and imposing; among its younger members, it was known as the Mausoleum. A porter greeted him.

'Would you like your car put away, sir?'

'No, thanks. I'd like a taxi.'

'At once, sir?'

'No, in a quarter of an hour.'

'I'll see to it.'

'Thanks, George,' said Dawlish. 'Have it at the back entrance, will you? The kitchen entrance.'

'The—the *kitchen* entrance?'

'That's it. And another thing. Any time now a man may come into the club and ask about me. He'll probably say he has to leave a message for the big fellow with the corn-coloured hair and the broken nose, or some such nonsense. Tell him the truth. You've heard the ridiculous stories about me, haven't you?'

'Some of them, sir.'

'Think up some more. Let him know what a devil I am when roused. And while you're doing this, take careful note of his face, his voice, and his clothes. Remember all the details you can, and let me know. When he's gone, put 'em down on paper. Don't forget that taxi either, will you?'

Dawlish strode blithely towards the marble staircase, whistling softly. He went into a booth and made two telephone calls—one to his friend Ted Beresford, the second to Timothy Jeremy.

When he emerged, he seemed cheerful. He looked down from the library floor, where he could see George; George was talking to a small man with dark hair and carrying a bowler hat.

The driver of the little car had worn a bowler.

Dawlish went into the kitchen. There, several cooks and the chef looked up with startled astonishment. He passed huge dishes of peeled potatoes, larger ones of cabbage, and a number of joints of meat in their dishes and prepared for the oven, and walked to a door leading to a narrow side street. Outside, a taxi was waiting.

Ten minutes saw him in another narrow street, in the West End of London. Here were many small shops, and few were devoted to ordinary trade.

He entered a gunsmith's.

A small, old man sitting behind a high desk, looked up and smiled as if with real pleasure.

'Hallo, James. You keeping well?'

'Not so bad for an old 'un, sir. Eighty-one last March, I was, sir, but I keep going. Can't abear doing *nothing*.' James smoothed down the few grey hairs on a nearly bald pate, and put on a pair of pince-nez. Behind him were guns of all kinds and descriptions, in racks which looked as old as the owner himself. 'What can I do for *you*, sir?'

'I've come about some keys.'

'*Keys?*'

'These keys,' said Dawlish, pushing them towards the old one. 'They're Chaldon door and Chaldon safe keys, and I want them copied. I know this is a gunsmith's, but I don't know any locksmiths I can trust. I don't want everyone to know that I'm going to do a spot of burglary, do I?'

'Naturally not,' said James, after a pause.

'In fact, I don't want the keys to be the same as these; I just want them to *look* the same. And can I have them by five o'clock this afternoon?'

'Well—perhaps—'

'I knew I could rely on you,' said Dawlish gratefully.

Dawlish lounged inside a telephone booth, from which he could see Helen. It was five minutes past six, and the underground station at Piccadilly was crowded. Many dawdled, waiting for friends, and stood in little groups, talking—sometimes laughing. Here and there a boy met girl, and they kissed fondly.

Helen stood a few yards away from Dawlish, but didn't notice him, because he wore an old cloth cap and a choker, and, by bending his knees, concealed his height. Helen was pale. Whenever a man drew near her, she stiffened and clutched her handbag tightly. She wore a black suit, and a small hat with a gaudy bunch of cherries in the middle.

Man after man passed her. The minutes ticked by.

Then the man in the bowler hat appeared.

He was spruce and dapper, with a wasp waist and squared shoulders, and he walked briskly. When Helen saw him, she flinched. The man's expression didn't alter. He was neither good- nor bad-looking, just a bundle of efficiency, to judge from his appearance. He went straight up to Helen, and spoke.

Dawlish watched her mouth.

She framed a word: 'Yes.'

The man thrust out his hand, and spoke again. She opened her bag, took out a small brown-paper packet, and gave it to him. She didn't speak again. The man leaned forward and gripped her arm, saying something which Dawlish couldn't hear. Still Helen didn't speak; there was no doubt of her terror.

The man pulled at her arm.

She opened her mouth, as if to scream—and then another man appeared, a remarkable fellow, for he was as large as Dawlish; he looked even bigger. He was dressed as a labourer, and reeled from side to side, as if he were drunk. He knocked against the man in the bowler hat, sending him into Helen. The man swung round, releasing the girl—and quick as a flash she darted away and was swallowed up in the crowd. The man in the bowler hat appeared to say harsh things to the labourer, who grinned at him vacantly.

Dawlish stepped out of the telephone booth.

He kept his knees bent, so as to lose two inches of his height. He heard the labourer, who was really Ted Beresford, say:

'Hic! Sorry, I'm sure. Hic.'

'You clumsy fool. You're drunk. I'll have the police—'

'Sho sorry,' said the labourer. 'I apologise.' He touched his cap. 'Goo' night.' He grinned again, as vacantly, and walked unsteadily away, but he did not go in the same direction as Helen.

Nor did the man in the bowler hat.

He pocketed the packet without examining the contents, and walked briskly to the Regent Street exit. Dawlish followed him. He stopped in the first doorway, took out the packet, and opened it. At sight of the keys, he gave a light tight-lipped smile, straightened his bowler, and then began looking for a taxi. Several passed him.

One, with the flag down, drew near to Dawlish.

'Cab, sir?'

'On the dot, as usual,' said Dawlish. 'Thanks. You see that little fellow trying to get a cab?'

'Yep!'

'Follow him, Bert,' said Dawlish.

'Sure,' said the cabby, as Dawlish sank bank in his seat. 'Long time since I done a job for you, Mr. Dawlish. Got quite a kick when I had your message.' He gave a clucking laugh. 'He's got one, guv'nor.'

Oxford Circus; Portland Place; Regent's Park. They went bowling along the road towards Maida Vale, then turned to the left. Not far along, the first taxi stopped. Dawlish saw that it was outside a tall, square, ugly house. It needed painting, and the garden was overgrown.

'Okay 'ere?' asked his driver.

'Yes, pull up just round the corner, where you can keep your eyes on this gate. If I'm more than an hour, Mr. Beresford will relieve you.'

It was now half-past six, and broad daylight; darkness would not fall for nearly two hours. People and traffic were sparse.

Dawlish turned into the gateway, and saw that the number 21 was painted on the gatepost. He murmured aloud: '21, Elkin Street,' as he approached the front door. It was reached by climbing eight wide, stone steps, and on either side of a large porch was a square pillar.

Seen through the windows, the downstairs rooms looked drab and old. The front door had once been painted green, but was now blistered and flaked.

Dawlish tried the door. He didn't expect to find it open; but it was.

He stepped inside a hall which was little more than a passage. On one side was a massive hallstand, empty of hats and coats. Opposite was a large framed print, its glass cracked, depicting a Highland scene where shaggy cattle stood by a tumbling, mountain burn. At the end of the passage was a door; and by the door, a staircase. The name on the door nameplate was 'Grey.' He went up to the next landing, and realised that each floor had been turned into a self-contained flat. There were four.

He decided to try each flat, starting at the top. Here, the front door was freshly painted, a new and modern lock had been fitted recently, and the brass of knocker, bell, and letter-box shone.

He pressed the bell, and heard it ring inside the flat.

Almost immediately, a door opened and he heard footsteps. Someone called out in a thin voice: 'If it's Mobey, tell him to come back in an hour.' The last word came most clearly, for the door opened on them, and a pale-faced man with dark hair stood in front of Dawlish. On his forehead was a red ridge, where his bowler hat had pressed.

CHAPTER VII

THE SQUARE ROOM

'I've come about the gas,' said Dawlish.

'What gas?'

'Don't you have gas here?' asked Dawlish. He straightened up, and the restless eyes became still in astonishment, for a tall man had suddenly become a giant.

Recognition flared together with anger, but there was no hint of fear.

Dawlish thrust the man back, not roughly, but with the deliberate strength of a tank crushing a brick wall. 'I'm sorry I'm not Mobey, but I think I want the same thing—a talk with you.'

They were now inside a tiny hall, a little more than a cubicle. A passage led from it, to the right; a door, ajar, was immediately behind the man whom Dawlish still held. The door didn't move, but there was a creak, as of a stealthy footstep.

He shifted his grip to the top of the arm, twisted, then whirled the man round so that he was in front of him, held fast by a half-Nelson.

The door didn't open any farther, but there was another stealthy sound. The man in Dawlish's grip back-heeled, and caught him painfully on the shin. Dawlish didn't relax his grip; instead, he tightened it, bringing a gasp. The creak came again, farther away—to his right. The passage led that way, and—yes, there was another door, leading from the room ahead to this passage. Dawlish grinned, as if he were greatly enjoying himself, and shifted position again. The victim now faced the passage and the far door.

A man's hand, then his face, appeared as he looked round. When he saw Dawlish staring at him over the dark head, he made no attempt to conceal himself, but came forward.

He had a gun.

'What's all this?'

The man Dawlish was holding spoke in a sighing voice.

'It's Dawlish.'

The other backed a pace, and lowered the gun towards the floor. Dawlish changed his grip swiftly, placed his right hand between the little man's shoulder blades, and shot him forward. Out of the medley of whirling arms and staggering bodies he selected the gun. He plucked it away, put it in his pocket and stood back, surveying the scene.

Behind the men were three doors. First, that from which the second man had appeared, leading to the left; opposite it, two others. He thrust the first door wide open, and found a bath-room. Before either of the others could resist, he bundled them inside, took the key from the inside of the door and locked them in, leaving the key in the lock.

He stepped into the room from which the second man had come.

It was large and square, and there were three big windows, overlooking the street. The furniture was modern, and there wasn't much of it. A faint grey haze of blue tobacco smoke filled the room, and there was a smell of Turkish tobacco.

On a desk were the keys, a manilla folder, and several letters addressed to 21d, Elkin Street, one to William Steen, and four to Jacob Martson. Not Marston; Martson. He went back to the passage and stood outside the bathroom door.

The men were muttering together.

He opened the other door. It led to a kitchen, and beyond was another passage; off this were three bedrooms, all furnished in severe modern style, all empty. He looked in the wardrobes and under the beds, but no one else was in the flat. The one room which held his attention longer than the others was a woman's bedroom. Everything on the dressing-table was expensive; the make-up came from a small exclusive Bond Street shop called *Lida*.

Dawlish went back to the front door, and shot the top and bottom bolts. Then he returned to the big square room. At one side a large electric fire was built into the wall, and in front of it were two arm-chairs.

He pulled a chair up to the desk and ran through the papers and letters. Most of them dealt with business orders, and the orders were all for *toys*. In the folder were orders for large quantities of small playthings. There was a column for the price and another for the purchase tax on several invoices.

Next, he went through all the papers in the desk, looking for mention of Jeremiah, Lord Calder. He didn't find one; nor did he find a reference to Helen Graves or Mick Ryan.

He found a small ledger, labelled: '*Commission Salesmen*'. He opened it, and found an index, where seventeen names were listed, opposite each name the word '*zone*'. The zone marked *London, Central*, had the names of three salesmen. Numerous entries showed what seemed to be the amount of commission they had been paid during the last eighteen months.

The first entries were dated eighteen months ago, against the names of twelve of the seventeen salesmen; the others started at different times, and the last salesman had been receiving commission only since the beginning of March, this year.

This salesman's name was Benson.

Dawlish made a pencil note of Benson's address, as well as the addresses of the three London and two Home Counties salesmen. Towards the end of his researches, he heard stealthy movements. He closed the book quietly, and put it back in the drawer. He closed the drawer as a sharp creak broke the still silence of the square room.

He lit a cigarette, and said:

'Hallo? Picked the lock already? Where do you keep your beer?'

He turned to see Steen—or was it Martson?—standing in the doorway with a long broom in his hand. Behind him Martson—or was it Steen?—hovered with a glinting table knife.

'Put away the implements, and come and sit down,' invited Dawlish. 'We ought to talk this over.'

The man threw the knife.

Dawlish dodged. The knife actually touched his cheek; he felt it, more sting than pain. It hit the far wall and clattered noisily against the chromium steel of an arm-chair. And as it fell the tall man came rushing forward with the broom raised.

Dawlish pushed the head of the broom aside, scratching his hand on the bristles, and Martson—or was it Steen?—staggered towards him, carried on by the impetus of his own rush. Dawlish thrust him back *and* stood up, and leaned against the desk, massive and towering. His old tweed suit and the choker suggested he might be a docker or a navvy. 'Which of you is Steen?' he asked cheerfully.

'I am,' said the stocky man. He showed no sign of fear, but the tall Martson did.

'Now I can tell Martson from Steen,' said Dawlish. 'All we want now is Mobey. Did Mobey kill Ryan?'

'I've never known of anyone called Ryan. If you think you can put anything over on us, you've another think coming. We'll have the police on you. We'll show you—'

'Don't be silly,' said Dawlish patiently. 'And come and sit down.'

He indicated the chairs nearest him, and after a pause they obeyed. Martson gripped the arm of his chair and seemed to become increasingly nervous. Steen was impassive.

'Did Mobey kill Ryan?' repeated Dawlish.

'We don't know who you're talking about,' said Steen.

'Why did you want Lord Calder's keys?'

Steen said: 'How the hell—' and then broke off.

Martson licked his lips nervously.

Steen said hoarsely: 'I'll murder that girl!'

Dawlish lunged towards him, grabbed his coat and pulled him out of the chair, then shook him violently.

'You won't murder anyone. If anything happens to Helen Graves, you'll answer for it to me. If you want to keep the police out of this, leave Helen alone.'

Then a new voice came from the door—a woman's voice.

The woman who came in slowly was tall and lovely; the gun in her hand seemed like a toy.

'So nice of you not to send for the police right away,' she said. 'We all appreciate it.'

She smiled at him—and Steen leapt out of his chair and darted at Dawlish.

CHAPTER VIII

THE BEAUTY

Dawlish could have sent Steen flying back, but didn't trouble. Steen dived a hand into Dawlish's pocket, drew out the gun and backed quickly away. When he saw Dawlish's blank expression, he moved forward again and drove his fist into Dawlish's face.

Dawlish turned his head and took the blow on the temple. He didn't look at Steen, and his very impassiveness discouraged a further blow.

Dawlish looked at the woman and beamed; but his heart thumped.

'Why, hallo,' he said. 'Fancy seeing you.'

Steen snapped: 'Kate, do you know Dawlish?'

'I think I'd like to,' said Kate. She gave a low-pitched laugh, as if she were really amused, opened a small leather handbag and dropped her gun into it. Then she moved gracefully across the room. She was a rare and lovely creature, tall yet not stately. Her lips were ripe and red, her eyes blue-violet, shaded by the brim of her big hat. She wore a sleek-fitting tailor-made suit of black, with white at the cuffs and throat; her white blouse was fastened high at the neck.

'What a wonderful liar you are,' smiled Dawlish. 'Sorry if I've put my foot in it.' He sat on the desk, with his feet flat on the floor. 'Let's pretend we're strangers, then.'

'Kate—' began Steen.

'If you have to believe him, believe him,' said Kate. She wasn't at all put out; rather was she amused. 'What's going on, Mr.—Dawlish, is it?'

'And to think you used to call me Pat,' said Dawlish reproachfully. 'But if we must be formal—Dawlish it is. I was paying a social call and collecting some keys which Steen borrowed from a friend of mine.'

Kate's gaze turned towards the keys. Eagerness sprang into her eyes.

'And now Steen's going to take them from you,' she said. 'Dawlish—oh, *Dawlish*! Isn't this the man you were talking about, William, whose club-steward gave him such a glowing reference?'

'Yes,' said Steen.

'And the man whom Ryan wanted to see,' said Kate.

Dawlish murmured: 'Mistake, Kate. They don't know anyone called Ryan. Ask them.'

'Perhaps they were just stalling,' said Kate. She drew near to Dawlish and picked up the keys, tossed them in the air and caught them, and gave a little laugh. 'Thanks. What have you done to your hand?'

'Mobey did that, last night.'

'Mobey was here all last night!' snapped Steen, and so gave the truth away. 'Stop wasting time, Kate. We've got to decide what to do.'

'That need not take long,' said Martson, coldly. 'Come away from the desk, Dawlish.' When Dawlish didn't obey, he pushed him; it was like pushing an elephant. Steen turned the gun in his hand, and brought the butt down sharply towards the back of Dawlish's injured hand. Dawlish snatched his hand away, swung his right arm, and crashed the fist on to Steen's jaw. The man's feet actually left the floor as he went backwards.

Kate's eyes seemed to glow.

'How strong he is!'

'Get off that desk!' screeched Martson. 'Kate! Make him get off.'

But Dawlish paid no attention to him or to Kate, just looked at Steen. The man was still on the floor, resting on one elbow, and pointing the gun. He sat up, still covering Dawlish.

Dawlish steeled himself to spring—backwards or sideways, anywhere out of the line of fire. But those glaring, glittering eyes suggested that whichever way he moved, Steen would get him. Dawlish swayed a little to the right.

'Not here, you fool!' snapped Kate.

'Right here and now,' grated Steen. 'And you aren't going to stop me.' He got up; the gun kept steady in his hand.

Kate took two quick steps, and stood between Dawlish and the gun.

'Not here,' she repeated. 'Don't lose your head, Steen. You can do what you like with him later, but not here.'

Martson licked his lips.

'Steen—'

'You ruddy fool! Kill him while we've got the chance. He'll go straight to the police if he gets away. He's been getting at Helen Graves, hasn't he? And why do you think Ryan went to see him?'

'He's right, Kate, the quicker—'

'What good *are* men?' asked Kate impatiently. She stepped

aside. 'All right, William, get it over—and don't blame me when you wish you hadn't.'

The gun was steady as a rock.

'What do you mean?' squeaked Martson.

'Do we know why Ryan went to Dawlish? Do we know how much he knows, what else he's done, whether he's actually seen the police or not? Kill him, and we'll never know.' She took off the huge hat, held it by her side, and poked the fingers of her free hand through her hair. 'Go on, finish it off.'

Steen didn't shoot.

Martson stood undecidedly, and Dawlish stood impassively by the desk. The lust to kill was still in Steen's eyes.

Kate went towards the corner door which led to the bedrooms.

'Don't ask me to help getting that carcase outside,' she said. 'Ask him how much he weighs!' She gave a little mirthless laugh, opened the door and went out.

'She's right,' said Martson slowly. 'We'd better wait, Steen.'

Dawlish didn't wait to be told again, but moved away from the desk. The strain had told on him; he was glad to lower himself into a chair, and thankful he'd been able to keep a poker face. Murder had been postponed because it suited their purpose, and because Kate had realised that. A phrase kept turning in his mind, like words printed on a revolving wheel. '*I owe my life to Kate, I owe my life to Kate.*'

Martson had resumed control. 'Where *is* Mobey? Why isn't he here? No one is ever here when I want them.' He looked at the papers on the desk. 'Did you look inside the desk, Dawlish?'

'What do you think he did?' sneered Steen. 'Trimmed his finger-nails or had a little nap?'

Steen had accepted the decision, but was sore.

'Did you look inside the desk?' asked Martson, smoothly. 'Answer me, Dawlish, or you'll get hurt.'

'Yes.'

'What did you see?'

'No children,' said Dawlish.

Steen bent down, picked up the broom, and thrust the hard bristles into Dawlish's face. Some stung his eyes, others scratched his cheek.

Steen took the broom away. Dawlish felt a little trickle of blood: his face smarted; his eyes watered freely.

'What do you mean, children?' demanded Martson in the same calm, menacing voice.

'Don't you deal in toys?'

Steen said slowly, softly: 'Maybe he's not so clever.'

'He's clever enough,' said Kate.

She had a knack of silent movement and appearing out of the blue. She'd tidied her hair which was a dark and gleaming mass of waves, and looked vividly, vitally alive.

'I've just telephoned Helen, and heard a most interesting story,' said Kate. 'I think we ought to think twice before we do away with Patrick Dawlish. He's friendly with the police, and has fooled them over this. I wonder why?' She answered the question herself. 'He knows there's big money in it, but I shouldn't think he'll be greedy. What kind of a cut do you want, Dawlish?'

Steen said in a strangled voice: 'Dawlish doesn't get any cut!'

'A quarter?' asked Kate, ignoring him.

Here was a game Dawlish could play; a deadly blindman's bluff. He might even convince them that he would really become a partner in their foul game.

'That doesn't seem very much.' He took out his cigarettes, while Steen watched, lynx-eyed. Blood from a scratch was sticky on his lips, and the cigarette was daubed red, as with a lipstick; but he lit it. 'And I'd have to have a lot of guarantees before I did a deal with Comrade Steen. Or Professor Martson, if it comes to that. But you're different, Kate.'

CHAPTER IX

THE MAN IN MARTSON

Something had happened to Martson.

'Not twenty-five per cent—I couldn't hear of it,' Martson said. 'I don't know what you're thinking about, Kate. Twenty-five per cent, indeed! Ten—well perhaps ten. Of course, it depends on whether Dawlish could do anything to help.'

'Do you hear that, Dawlish?' said Kate.

'You're crazy,' said Steen. 'I won't do any kind of deal with Dawlish. I don't trust him. I don't give a damn what Helen told you. She's a born liar. Just find out what Dawlish knows and then cut his throat.'

'You talk too much,' said Martson sharply. 'I won't have you interfere in this matter; it's my province. You do what you're told.' No doubt now who was the leader here. 'Dawlish, I *might* give you ten per cent if you are honest with us. But you must be honest.'

Dawlish kept his face expressionless

'What's your offer?'

'Tell us just what you know, how you propose to set about it, what plans you have made. Tell us everything, Dawlish; let us see whether we can talk business.'

'If I do a deal, it'll be on a fifty-fifty basis,' Dawlish said.

'An even split? Ridiculous! Look at the risk we've already taken. Look at what we've already done. You would have known nothing about it if Ryan hadn't come to see you. And you don't know everything. You can't—because Ryan didn't get to you in time.'

'I know plenty.'

'You know a little, and—well, I'll admit you might be useful to us. Might be. I think there are a lot of trifling things that you could do, but we should have to do the real work. We have everything ready—we're just ready to move as soon as the annoying oddments are cleared up. Fifteen—well, I *might* consider fifteen per cent.'

'Fifty,' repeated Dawlish stonily.

'Dawlish, you are only wasting time with this nonsense. Fifteen per cent—at the very most, twenty.'

'Supposing you let Dawlish think it over?' suggested Kate smoothly. 'He has everything to gain.'

'I like to decide quickly. But I see your point, my dear. Perhaps Dawlish will, if he has time for contemplation. All right, he may have a few hours to think it over. But not here—we can't keep him here. We'll take him—'

'I'll look after him,' said Kate.

Steen swung round from the window. 'You'll what?'

'Very well, very well, take him away,' said Martson, as if Steen hadn't spoken. 'I have a lot to do, and Mobey hasn't arrived yet.'

He looked down at the papers on his desk, and seemed to withdraw into another world.

Kate touched Dawlish's arm.

'Don't be difficult, will you?'

'With you, pet? Never!'

Hate and suspicion were back in Steen's eyes.

'We'll put it to the test,' said Kate. She opened her handbag, and Dawlish saw the little gun nestling in it. She took out a small glass phial. She uncorked it, and shook two tablets out on to the gloved palm of her hand. 'Take these, Dawlish. They won't hurt you. They'll just send you to sleep for an hour or two. You won't even have a hang-over.'

Dawlish took them in his fingers.

There was a challenge in Kate's smiling eyes. Steen, farther away, was menacing. Martson didn't look up. An age seemed to pass in the next few seconds. Were these tablets harmless? Would she have gone to so much trouble, only to poison him? Bert the taxi-driver or Ted Beresford were watching the house. If he were taken away, he would be followed. But Kate and Steen would go to a lot of trouble to throw off pursuit.

But why weigh up the pros and cons? Either try to escape now, or take the tablets quietly.

Kate and Steen had a gun apiece, but Dawlish had only to stretch out his hand, swing Kate round and get her gun. A split second could turn the odds in his favour. He was nearer the door than Steen or Martson—bad tactics on their part.

Why not take this chance, instead of taking the risk with the tablets?

Because of a dead youth, whom he'd never seen in life? Of a girl he didn't trust? Because of some unknown crime planned against an eccentric millionaire, whom he'd never seen either?

He seemed to see the burn scars on Mick Ryan's body.

Dawlish put the tablets into his mouth, and swallowed them.

He couldn't do anything about it now—and the fear that he might go to sleep and never wake up brought him near to panic. He fought against it, steeling himself to keep a poker face as he looked at Kate.

'Now go and sit down,' ordered Kate.

He obeyed.

But the drug wouldn't act for some minutes, and his chance of turning the tables was much greater now. They thought he'd swallowed bait as well as tablets. An hour or two hours? He wanted to close his eyes, and stifled a yawn. He mustn't go to sleep. Idiot! That's exactly what he would have to do, why he had been given the tablets. They'd taken effect more quickly than he'd expected, and any chance of attacking was rapidly diminishing. In a few seconds it would be gone.

Kate stood in front of him, although he hadn't noticed her move.

'Come with me,' she said.

His legs felt numbed as he stood up, although his mind was clear enough. He yawned. Kate took his arm and held it tightly; warm softness pressed against his hand. She looked at him, as she might at a lover.

Steen opened the front door.

The stairs seemed to come up and meet him; he wouldn't have managed to get down without Kate's help.

A gleaming new two-seater stood outside. Kate helped him in. Yawning, he watched her walk round the car and take the wheel. All her movements were flowing and graceful.

'Lean back and close your eyes.'

He obeyed, and when they turned into the road, didn't open his eyes again to see whether Beresford or the taxi-driver were watching. He didn't notice traffic sliding by, or hear any sound except in the distance.

He head lolled to one side, and rested on Kate's shoulder.

He didn't see her smile.

CHAPTER X

THE BACK STREET

It was raining.

Dawlish was aware of that in a vague way. He didn't open his eyes. He was lying down, felt warm and pleasantly drowsy, and was unaware of anything that had happened in the past day or two.

What time was it? Was it daylight? He ought to know whether it was time to get up. Whether Felicity—

She stirred by his side.

He murmured: 'Time we got up, sweet?'

She didn't answer, yet she was usually awake before he was. So perhaps it wasn't time to get up. No, of course it wasn't, this was night-time. Dawn? The birds always greeted the dawn, and they weren't doing so now. Probably about half-past five.

His left hand hurt—a sharp, throbbing pain shot across it, red-hot and vicious as he turned.

His body went rigid; for he remembered. He was waking from a drugged sleep, and he'd thought that Felicity was by his side.

Someone was.

He opened his eyes. As he was lying on his back, all he saw

53

was the ceiling and the window, opposite the bed. It was an old-fashioned iron bedstead, black enamelled. The window overlooked a grey wall, blank, drab, dark, and sightless; silly thought, a sightless wall. That was a view he was used to.

There were curtains at the window. A wash-stand, with a huge jug and bowl and a marble top. Two chairs—and folded over one of the chairs, his clothes.

He remembered getting into the car and letting his head fall on Kate's shoulder, and even that was vague. He had no idea how long ago that was or where he was now, or who was beside him. There was a musty smell, too, as if the room and all that was in it was thick with dust. The bedspread, a quilted thing of many colours, was dirty and torn.

Next to his own feet where they made a lump against the counterpane, was another lump.

He moved his legs a little; and felt the familiar and yet so different touch. The warm, cosy touch of smooth skin.

He looked round, slowly and deliberately, expecting to see Kate.

Helen lay staring at him.

Her eyes were dazed, she looked pale and tired, but the strain which he'd seen before had gone. Her dark hair was like a canopy over her pillow. Her mouth was slack and red at one corner; as if she had been dribbling; yes, there was a damp patch. She looked at him bewilderedly—as he looked at her.

One bare shoulder showed above the bedclothes.

His hand throbbed, his head throbbed, and his heart beat sickeningly. This was something too deep for comprehension. It was hard even to acknowledge that he was here, with her. There was something else wrong, too; with himself. He wouldn't normally feel or act like this, his reaction would be different— he shouldn't be feeling coy and bashful, because—

She flung the bedclothes back suddenly, moved—and then pulled them over her again. A red flush crept over her face and neck.

He said: 'I don't know how it happened, either. Did they drug you?'

'I—yes!'

'And me. They're having a heck of a laugh somewhere, my poppet, but I shouldn't worry too much. Turn your back, will you? Then I can put some clothes on,' said Dawlish.

She turned round, convulsing the bedclothes, and Dawlish sat up. On the wall by the side of the bed was a long mirror, and he saw first his face, scratched but cleaned, and his powerful chest red but not a bit like Mick Ryan's. He pushed the bedclothes back, and didn't look at Helen as he went to the chair and dragged on his pants and singlet.

He ran a finger over his stubble; his chin was sore. His mouth was parched. He dressed—except for his coat and tie, for it was muggy-warm in here.

The window was tightly closed. He opened it a little and the rain splashed gently on to his face, welcome and refreshing. He breathed in the cooler air, and stared at the wall—a window-less wall—opposite him. It seemed to stretch unending in each direction. He leaned forward and looked down. He was on the third or fourth floor of a house, and below him was a narrow, asphalt-paved path or alley.

He went to the door, and tried it; it was locked.

Helen said: 'What—what are we going to do?'

'Sort things out,' said Dawlish. He felt that he was fit enough to try, anyhow.

He looked at his watch. It was twenty-five minutes past seven—morning. He'd been here, or at least he'd been uncon-scious, for the better part of twelve hours. A lot of things could happen in twelve hours, but—one thing couldn't. Steen and Martson hadn't found the genuine keys.

'We can't stay here! Open the door, go away, go away and—' Helen's voice trailed off.

'That's the trouble, what are we going to do after that?' asked Dawlish. 'On the whole, I think we'd be wise to wait for something to turn up. They've left you your clothes. Be grateful for small mercies.'

He looked out of the window again.

He was aware of little sounds behind him, springs creaking, the chair moving, clothes rustling. But gradually they faded, for there were sounds farther away, familiar and comforting. People were walking; he wasn't far from a busy thoroughfare. And something else—a mournful hoot, which he recognised; a tug or small boat, on the river.

He heard Helen move behind him, but didn't turn round. The handle of the door rattled.

'It really is locked,' he said, and looked at her.

She stood by the door, hopelessness on her face as she tugged at the handle.

'Who—who brought *you* here?' she asked.

'A friend of yours. Kate.'

'*Kate!*'

'Who brought you?' he asked.

She shivered. 'I—I came.'

'So you know where we are?'

'Yes,' she said dully, 'I know where we are, but what difference does it make? There's nothing we can do while we're here. I knew—I knew I ought to have got away with the keys and handed them over. If only you hadn't taken them away from me. They'll kill us when they know they're false ones.'

Dawlish said: 'It might be some time before they find out.

They'll need time to plot and plan their raid on Jeremiah's vaults.'

She wasn't convinced; and that didn't matter. He looked into the china jug, but it was empty. There was no carafe or glass and of course there was no running water in the room.

He could break the door down, with little trouble but a lot of noise. He might be able to pick the lock, without it being heard, but if he did that—what then? Escape? He hadn't let himself be brought here so that he should escape without making any progress. The game had only just started. The trick with Helen had been intended to jolt him severely; a crafty, cunning, clever trick—almost certainly Kate's.

Both he and Helen were badly compromised; if anyone learned about it—

He shut that question out; of course, Kate knew and so did her boy friends. They might use this incident to exert pressure on him. But he knew that he would have to stay here, he couldn't escape until he knew more about this business.

He could help Helen to escape, but—would that be wise? He had little doubt that she was near hysteria again—real hysteria, now. But was it real? Was she capable of acting this part, so as to deceive him, lure him into talking?

He looked at her narrowly.

'*We must get away!*' She almost hissed the words.

'Oh, yes,' said Dawlish. 'I—'

He stopped, and listened intently—and heard footsteps on the stairs. They were slow, deliberate footsteps.

CHAPTER XI

BREAKFAST FOR TWO

The footsteps stopped; something clinked, sounding like a cup and saucer. He went to the bed and sat down, facing the door.

Helen came to him and clutched his arm.

'Here's our chance!'

Metal fidgeted against metal as the key was thrust in the door, and crockery rattled again. Then a man called out in a quavering voice:

'Open the door, please, open the door.'

'*Don't!*' gasped Helen, and shrank away. 'It's a trick, they might do anything.'

'Take it easy,' said Dawlish, and got up and opened the door wide.

A little old man with a completely bald head blinked at him. The new-comer had a face like a moulting owl, and was so nervous that the large tray shook in his hands, yet under the surface Dawlish suspected a vicious ruthlessness. He looked as if he would drop the tray with a crash, spilling tea, toast, milk, sugar, and whatever was under the two large china dish-covers.

'Good morning!' said Dawlish, cheerily.

'G-g-good morning,' stammered the man.

Behind him moved two men. They were shadowy figures, pressing into a corner almost out of sight, ready to deal with him if he rushed out.

'Put it on the dressing-table,' said Dawlish.

The old man staggered across the room, bowed down by the weight of the tray. He dumped the tray down, making everything rattle, and said that it wasn't much of a morning.

'Shocking,' agreed Dawlish. 'But I'm famished. What have you got?' He lifted a cover.

Bacon; two eggs; tomatoes; fried potatoes. It was appetising to look at and to smell, almost enough to make him forget to glance out of the room. One of the shadowy men was now by the door. Probably he couldn't really believe that Dawlish could be so tame.

Helen dashed forward, pushing Dawlish and the old man aside, reached the door, and sprang on to the landing. Dawlish called: 'Come back!' One of the men materialised, shot out a hand and grabbed her wrist. He was a whippet of a man.

Helen screamed, with shock as much as with pain.

The man didn't speak, but swung her round and pushed her roughly into the room. The old man backed hastily away, and came up against the bed. The glitter in his eyes as he smacked Helen's face confirmed all Dawlish thought of him. Helen flung herself on to the bed, burying her face in her hands. She began to cry, harshly, bitterly. The old man said: 'Silly slut,' and slapped her again before he went out.

'You know, my pet, you cry too much, and remind me of the man who protests too much,' said Dawlish unfeelingly. 'I'm hungry. If you take my advice, you won't let this get cold.'

He cleared the dressing-table, took the tray to it, and started to eat. The food was as good as it looked; even the tea was hot. He didn't glance in her direction, although he knew that she was peering at him through her fingers.

He beckoned.

She straightened up, and pushed the hair out of her eyes. She really had been crying, for tears stained her cheeks. But she came forward, pulled up a chair, and began to eat as if she were really hungry. Now and again she sniffed.

'If you'd tried to get away—' she began.

'It would have been asking for trouble. Anyhow, I want to talk to you. After all, we've spent a night together—that ought to put you in a confiding mood. Where are we?'

'Limehouse. Killiger Street—number 41. Not far from some docks.'

'Were you here before?'

'This is where they brought Mick.'

'How do you know?'

'He—he told me so.'

'And what made you come here?'

'They sent for me, when Mick was a prisoner. I didn't see any point in telling you. I saw Mick, just after that terrible day when they'd—they'd burnt him. That's why I'm so frightened. I can't help it, I'll do anything, *anything*, to be safe from them. I don't care what I do. Oh, I wish Mick had never come to see you! He'd be alive if he hadn't. They'd have the keys, everything would be all right. It wasn't *me* who killed Mick, it was you. It's your fault he's dead!'

'I know how you feel,' he said more gently. 'But you've got it all cock-eyed. Giving them the real keys won't help you. You'll always be in danger from them, unless I can come to an arrangement with them,' said Dawlish.

Something like horror crossed her face; and with it, contempt.

'So *that's* it! You're going to come to terms with them. And Mick thought he could trust you! You want to get something out of it, that's why you wouldn't tell the police, and you pretended it was for *my* sake.'

She swung round to the window and stood staring at the drab brick wall and the incessant rain.

For the first time, Dawlish began to trust her.

He said: 'If you take my advice, Helen, you won't try to get away, you'll just sit back and take what comes. You'll be all right if you do that.'

She didn't answer.

He felt in his breast pocket. His wallet was there, but not the slip of paper on which he'd written the names and addresses of the commission salesmen. He couldn't recall Benson's address, but later he might bring it to mind. In any case, he'd gone a long way since he had broken into the flat and sat at the desk in the square room. It was a good thing he'd played safe with the real keys, which were in a safe deposit; the key was at his club.

Footsteps sounded on the stairs again. The key turned in the lock, and the old man shuffled in, his little cruel eyes peering towards the tray.

'That's what I like to see, mister—empty plates. Nuffing like empty plates. Puts new life inter yer.' He winked. ''Ere, you,' he said, turning to Helen. 'Ahtside.'

She swung round.

'What do you mean?'

'There's a man wants ter see yer.'

She turned to Dawlish, hands outstretched, appealingly.

'Don't—don't let them—'

'It's all right,' said Dawlish. 'I'll come with you.'

'Oh, no, you won't!' snapped the old man.

Dawlish laughed. 'We'll see. Come on, Helen.'

He tucked her arm beneath his, and went to the door. There was a man outside the door; he appeared there as soon as Dawlish began to move. He also showed his gun.

'Come on, sweetie, he won't bite.'

The man was small, and wiry, and held the gun as if he were familiar with it. Dawlish stretched out a hand, quite gently, and pushed him aside, The man didn't shoot, but another appeared at the head of the stairs.

'Don't be silly,' said Dawlish. 'Where Helen goes, I go. You can't lock us together in a room and then expect us to be parted next morning.'

Helen dragged on his hand, and her fingers bit deeply into the flesh, hurting the wound; but he drew her onwards; only two feet separated him from the man at the head of the stairs.

The man backed down two steps.

Dawlish said: 'Hurry, old chap—I don't want to fall on you. I weigh too heavy.'

Someone else appeared on the landing below: Kate.

'Oh, hallo!' called Dawlish. 'Up bright and early? Tell this whipper-snapper that if he's not careful, I'll get cross, will you?'

The landing was in a half-light; Kate stood tall and still and very lovely—and smiling.

'All right, Ken,' she said, 'let him come too.'

The man shrugged his shoulders, put the gun away, and backed quickly down the stairs. Dawlish followed, with Helen a step behind him. Kate didn't move. A door was open behind her, and she said: 'In there.' Dawlish went into a sitting-room, larger than the bedroom. It might have been in any suburban house, being pleasantly furnished, but without much taste.

Steen said: 'I sent for the girl, not Dawlish.'

'And I was so tired of the bedroom I thought I'd come along,' said Dawlish. 'Sit down, Helen.' She nearly collapsed into a chair—and stared at Steen. All the fear she had known, had shown and felt, was centred on this man.

Steen said: 'Okay, you've had your walk. Now get back upstairs.'

Dawlish selected another arm-chair, and said: 'No, not just yet. I want to make one thing clear,' said Dawlish, and leaned forward earnestly. 'Steen, get this into your thick head. I might play. I'm not certain yet, but I might play. That'll mean a lot of things you don't realise. I can get the police off the hunt—I can put them on the wrong track quite easily. Understand? I can help in many ways, but—on one condition, and if you won't agree to it, we won't do any business.'

Steen wanted to tell him to hell with business; he hadn't lost his hatred.

Kate said: 'Don't be so melodramatic, Dawlish. What are you getting at?'

'A square deal for Helen,' said Dawlish. 'I don't like the way you've treated her. Stop doing it. She's to be released, to go free—and she's to stay free. Otherwise, no deal.'

Kate said: 'You've got a nerve.'

'I thought we agreed about that last night.'

'But things aren't the same as they were last night,' said Kate, and laughed softly. 'You've had a night out on the tiles. Look.'

She went to the desk, and Dawlish saw that Steen's lips curved in an ugly smile. There were some photographs on the desk—big, glossy ones, like those used by newspapers. They were upside down to him, and he waited until Kate held them out, the right way up.

They were photographs of him—and Helen. Together.

CHAPTER XII

DARK ROOM

Kate's eyes were brimming over with amusement.

'Aren't they good?' she asked.

'Wonderful,' said Dawlish evenly.

'So lifelike—you're both sleeping the sleep of exhaustion,' said Kate. 'We were afraid we'd wake you up when we put the lights on, but you didn't even stir at the flashlight. It was a little ticklish to adjust the bedclothes *quite* like that. Matey, isn't it? And it's shaken you,' said Kate. 'Not a bad idea, was it?'

'Brilliant.'

'I don't think you see the funny side of it,' said Kate chidingly. 'I wonder if you see the serious side, Pat *dear*.'

'Clearly.'

Kate shrugged her shoulders, and Steen said: 'Okay. Now go upstairs. We'll handle the girl the way we want to.'

'Oh, no,' said Dawlish. 'I knew there'd be something we'd fall out about. This is it. Helen's to be left alone, from now on.'

Kate frowned.

'I don't think you get it, Dawlish.'

'Oh, but I do. There's just one thing I can't stomach,' said

Dawlish. 'Watching people who are frightened—like Helen. You've got the keys. You've got Mick Ryan where you want him. Helen goes free. Or—'

'Felicity gets a photograph.'

'All right, Felicity gets a photograph,' said Dawlish. 'And other people get surprises.' He raised his hands and smiled broadly. 'You didn't expect me to walk into your parlour last night without taking some kind of safeguards, did you?'

Kate said: 'Phooey. Whatever you tried to do, didn't come off. You had a friend in a car round the corner—a Bentley. He had a slight accident. Not serious, he didn't come to any harm, but he didn't follow us far.' She laughed. 'And you had another friend, who was following Helen. He missed her at Piccadilly Circus. Do you see what I mean, Dawlish?'

Dawlish shrugged.

'I expected you to look after the obvious things.'

'And the police were watching Helen, but they also lost her,' said Kate. 'There was a detective from Haslemere and another from Scotland Yard. What a pity we knew who they were! Both were held up at the subway when Helen was making off—and Helen came straight here, because she was too frightened not to. There's a general call out for her—did you know that? The police are very anxious to find out where she is. Call it a day, Dawlish. Go upstairs, and leave the girl to us.'

Dawlish placed his hands on the arms of his chair, and sprang to his feet.

'All right,' he said. 'Come on, Helen, we're getting out of here.'

He pulled Helen from her chair.

They actually allowed him to reach the landing before they recovered from their astonishment. Had it been the ground instead of the first floor, he might have reached the street, although he didn't hurry, and kept a firm grip on Helen's arm.

A man appeared at the foot of the stairs; Ken, showing his gun again. There was another on the landing above, covering him from there. Steen rushed to the door, pushing past Kate—but Kate was able to look over his shoulder.

Steen rasped out: 'Dawlish, if you go down those stairs, you'll be shot.'

'All right, I'll be shot,' said Dawlish. 'Don't worry, Helen. Get behind me.'

He took a step forward.

'No!' gasped Helen. 'No, they mean it, they'll shoot if you go downstairs. Don't go. *Don't go!*'

'She's wise,' said Kate softly.

Steen took two steps forward. He was quivering with anger and with uncertainty. He didn't know what to expect next from Dawlish. He didn't know, either, the single characteristic which had made Dawlish so hard to beat. This was complete disregard of danger when he thought the moment ripe, and a mind which was prepared to startle and shock opponents, keeping them on the defensive even when they had the whip hand.

'Don't be a fool, Dawlish.' Kate's voice had a different ring—and proved the one thing that mattered: they didn't want to shoot. It wasn't just because they were afraid of making a noise; they didn't want to shoot *him*.

'Sorry, Kate,' he said. 'No sense in going on if we can't start off on the right foot. Come on, Helen.'

He stretched out a hand to take her arm.

She shrank back.

Steen stepped swiftly between her and Dawlish, doing the one thing Dawlish wanted. He brought his injured hand into play. Pain streaked through it, like a slash from a red-hot sword, but he grabbed Steen round the waist and lifted him—shoulder-high, head high, then above his head.

He hurled Steen down the stairs.

He didn't just drop him or let him bounce, but flung him through the air. Steen crashed into Ken at the foot of the stairs. As they fell, Dawlish went down four steps at a time, making the staircase and the landings shake. The man above daren't shoot, for he might hit any one of the three.

'*Run, Helen!*' roared Dawlish.

She stood trembling near the head of the stairs, as Dawlish reached the hall, saw Ken's gun lying against the wall, and picked it up. He turned. The man who had been at the top landing had reached the next, gun in hand. Dawlish fired; the gun dropped from the man's hand, hit the stairs and bounced down.

'Don't move, Kate,' called Dawlish. 'Come on, Helen!'

He didn't glance down or round, but knew that one of the men was stirring. Another was groaning. He backed a pace, then dared to glance behind him. Steen lay on his back, his face twisted in pain, his hands clenched. Ken was getting unsteadily to his knees. There was a dazed look in one eye; the other had closed right up and was swelling visibly.

Helen started down the stairs.

Kate stood like a Juno in black, her lovely face expressionless.

Helen reached Dawlish's side.

'Open the door,' he said. 'Be careful, there might be a guard outside.'

She stepped over Steen. Ken made no attempt to stop her, and swayed back against the wall, still on his knees. A bolt went back, the door creaked.

Helen whispered: 'No—no one's here.'

'Go into the street, look up and down, and call out if all's safe.'

Kate hurried into the sitting-room.

Helen called out in a strained voice: 'It's all right.'

Dawlish backed to the door, pulled it wider open, and took a last look at the two men on the floor and the man on the landing. He went out, slamming the door behind him; the bang echoed up and down the street. Helen stood in the pouring rain, her hair already plastered over her forehead; she was shivering.

He took her hand and they raced along the narrow street. There were terraced houses on one side and several low buildings on the other.

There was a shop at the second corner.

He pushed her against the door, and the inside bell clanged. No one was in the tiny shop, which was crammed with tinned and packet goods.

A door leading to the back of the shop opened and a pale-faced, plump young woman came out briskly.

'Strewth! Been out in the rain?'

'Silly, wasn't it? May we use your telephone?'

'Okay, s'in the corner.'

She pointed to a telephone

'Like a cup o' tea, duck?'

Dawlish was dialling and watching the window at the same time. 'That's a wonderful idea,' he said. 'Say yes, Helen.' The window was piled up with tins of soups and other things; three colourful towers with thick bases, ending in a one-tin pinnacle. Between them he could see into the street.

The ringing sound was in Dawlish's ears. The rain came down with steady, depressing persistence, streaking the window, rolling down in fits and starts.

A man was approaching; he could hear footsteps outside.

'Just made it, duck,' said the woman. 'Couldn't be served quicker in a cook shop, could yer?'

'Sanson's garrich,' a voice said into his ear.

'I want a cab, at once,' said Dawlish. 'My name is Dawlish, and I'm at the corner of Killiger Street, Limehouse, and I'm in a hurry.'

'Okay, Mr. Dawlish, be there right way. Ten minutes—'

Dawlish wiped perspiration off his forehead, and stepped into the shop. Helen was sipping her tea; the woman, with another large cup in her hand, stood behind the counter. She held the cup towards him.

'Save yer catching yer deaf,' she said.

'That's wonderful—you're very good.' As Dawlish took the cup, he heard Helen's clatter in the saucer. She was staring into the street. A face pressed against the window—the face of the man who had been on the landing, whose gun Dawlish had shot away. He drew back, and dodged out of sight.

'Steady, duck, don't drop it,' said the woman sharply; and frowned anxiously at Dawlish. 'No trouble is there?'

Dawlish sipped his tea. 'My friend's not well,' he said. 'Drink up, Helen.'

The cab wouldn't be here for ten minutes; ten minutes at least.

CHAPTER XIII

THE WOMAN WHO DIDN'T WANT TROUBLE

Another man appeared at the window; the old man, wearing a cap pulled low over his forehead. It didn't hide his beak of a nose or the top of his green baize apron.

'I don't want any trouble,' said the woman sharply.

Dawlish looked at and really saw her for the first time. She'd been handsome, in early youth. Although she was plump, there were scraggy lines at her throat. Her eyes were dark and troubled. She bulged in a pink blouse above a hessian apron tied tightly round a small waist.

Dawlish moved towards her, in full view of the window.

'I don't want to cause any,' Dawlish said. 'We're on the run. As soon as the cab arrives, we'll be off. Don't worry.'

'Don't worry!' she echoed, but was far too nervous to be sarcastic. 'I'm a n'onest woman, I am, never 'ad no trouble wiv the dicks. It's bad enough 'aving me old man inside, wivvaht you coming and causing trouble. Clear aht. You ain't no right to 'ide 'ere. If the rozzers—'

'We're not running from the police. A mob we've crossed. Know anyone named Steen—or Martson?'

'Never 'eard of 'em.'

'Let my friend come behind the counter, will you? Just look after her. You'll be all right.' He passed through the little gap in the counter, and the woman put out a hand, as if to hold him back, but didn't touch him. The room behind the shop was small and crammed with stock. One tall pile of cardboard boxes, close to the door, made a place behind which he could hide from both window and shop. A tea-pot and some dirty crockery stood on a small table beneath the window, which overlooked a narrow path, paved, wet, and greasy-looking, and the brick wall of a house. The gate at the end of the path was bolted from the inside with big shiny black bolts. There was also a door on the right of the room, leading to a passage.

Dawlish locked the door, and shifted a packing case in front of it. Then he saw a man climbing over the gate. It was Ken; his eye was closed right up. He dropped down lightly, and darted into a recess which Dawlish hadn't noticed; it hid him from the window.

Dawlish stepped behind the pile of boxes.

Helen screamed! The door of the shop burst open, making the bell jingle. Dawlish could see between the two cardboard boxes, into the shop. The old man came in, and the rain spattered the floor, in big dark spots.

The woman said: 'Shut up you. It's all right, Mr. Mulligan, I got a looney on me 'ands. Scared of 'er own shadow, she is. Wot—wot can I do for you to-day?'

'You don't want no trouble, Mrs. Bray, do you? The girl—' he looked at Helen, and also looked round the shop, as if expecting to see Dawlish spring up from the counter. 'She's up to no good. Done the dirty on some friends of mine. They want to see her, and she ran away wiv a man. Just let her come along wiv' me,

Mrs. Bray, and you won't 'ave no trouble. You've seen the man, 'aven't you? Run aht on 'er, that's what 'e's done.'

Dawlish looked at the back window.

Ken was sidling along the wall, gun in hand.

'I don't want no trouble, Mr. Mulligan, but that girl's got every right to stay 'ere, *if* she wants to.'

'Oh, no, she ain't,' said Mulligan the Owl. 'She's robbed a friend of mine, that's wot she's done. She's got to come along wiv me, Mrs. Bray.'

Ken was near the window now. Dawlish crouched against the corner, hidden by the boxes. He could only see Mulligan and Mrs. Bray: Helen had backed out of sight.

'If she wants to stay, she can stay!'

Ken had reached the window. He put his gun down, and began to push a screwdriver between the frame and the window-sill, to lever it up. He peered into the gloomy shop, nervously.

'I thought you never wanted no trouble, Mrs. Bray.' Mulligan's voice grated like an old parrot's. 'You'll get wot's coming to you if you get in the way. Nice little business you've got arahnd 'ere. Keeping it going until your ole man comes aht've clink. Think I don't know? Well, 'e won't 'ave no business to come back to, if you get in the way. Make the girl come aht to me.'

Ken had levered the window up far enough to get his fingers beneath it. Straining eyes, nerves, and muscles, he pushed it upwards, and climbed through. He knocked against the table and made the plates rattle.

'What's that?' gasped Helen.

'Don't you worry about little fings like that,' said Mulligan. Evil and menace rasped in his voice. ''And the skirt over, quick.'

'Get out of my shop!'

Ken was now in the doorway. Obviously he felt safe, for he squared his shoulders, and his final step was swaggering. He showed the woman his gun. Dawlish could only see the top of his head above the pile of cases.

'Okay, Mulligan,' Ken said. 'Take the skirt, and—'

Helen screamed, Mrs. Bray gasped, Mulligan raised his voice in sudden alarm. 'Put that dahn!' Something crashed into the glass of the window or the door. Ken swore and moved—and then Dawlish pushed the top case down. It touched Ken, who swung round—into Dawlish's hand, spread out and covering his face. Dawlish thrust him back against the side of the door; his head banged sickeningly.

There was another crash inside the shop.

Mulligan screamed: 'I'll bash your face in, you bitch!'

Dawlish rounded the pile of cases, hit Ken again, and took the gun away. Ken slumped down, unconscious. Dawlish stepped into the shop.

Helen was crouching just above the level of the counter. Mrs. Bray stood upright, two tins of food hugged to her breast, another poised in her right hand. Mulligan crouched near the door. Great white streaks spread from a hole in the window, and Mrs. Bray flung another tin at him. It missed by a yard, hit one of the towers, and brought a dozen tins crashing down. Others toppled slowly, then gradually fell more heavily. They made a constant undertone of sound, like distant thunder.

Mulligan grabbed the handle of the door, pulled it open and fled into the rain.

Mrs. Bray, her face turkey-red, put her tins down.

'All safe,' said Dawlish quietly. 'Thanks. I won't forget that.'

He took a piece of string from behind the counter, and tied Ken's hands; the man was just coming round.

'Coming into my shop and getting me into trouble like this! As if I 'aven't 'ad enough trouble, wiv me old man inside, and all this shop to manage on me own, no 'elp any time.'

'I'll put the damage right, and—'

'You never could put it right, not if you tried for a year. Mulligan will spread the word rahnd, I won't 'ave a customer, they won't dare come near the shop.'

A taxi pulled up outside.

'There's yer ruddy cab. Get aht! I don't want ter see you again. Get aht!' She ran at him, and pushed.

The driver—Bert, who had taken Dawlish to Elkin Street— was getting down from the wheel. Dawlish beckoned, and he came in, short, perky, with a clown's face and the steady eyes of a man who could be trusted in emergency. 'Helen, go in the cab, you'll be all right,' Dawlish said. 'Bert, take Miss Graves to Mr. Jeremy's flat. If Mr. Jeremy isn't in, wait with her until he arrives. If you're followed, stop and ask for police protection.'

'Okay. Come on, duckie.'

'It's all safe, Helen,' said Dawlish. He went with her and Bert to the door. There were no cars about, nothing to suggest that the taxi could be followed.

He opened the door, and the rain beat down on his face.

'Hurry, Bert. And keep an eye on her, she mustn't slip away.'

'It's the last fing I wanted, the very last fing I wanted,' muttered Mrs. Bray. 'I didn't want no trouble. Look wot you've done.' She surveyed the fallen tins, the shambles in the window and on the floor, the broken plate glass. Ken, still dazed, was squatting on the floor with his hands still tied behind his back, looking up at Dawlish. 'And it ain't only that. Mulligan will ruin me—'e won't let anyone come 'ere. They're all scared o' Mulligan.'

Dawlish said: 'I don't think Mulligan will come back. He's in too deep. If he does anything to interfere with your trade, I'll deal with him.'

'Anyone can talk,' she sniffed.

A car passed the corner, a sleek green two-seater. Dawlish recognised the car vaguely, the woman at the wheel vividly. Kate didn't look at the shop. Mulligan did: he crouched in the dicky seat, with a raincoat round his shoulders like a cape. Someone was leaning back next to Kate: Dawlish didn't see who it was.

He said: 'I'll keep in touch with you, and this will pay for the damage.' He put ten one-pound notes on the counter; he didn't want to overdo it at first; she would resent that. She didn't speak, and Dawlish went behind the counter and yanked Ken to his feet.

He unfastened Ken's wrists, held his arm tightly, and said: 'We're going to Mulligan's house. If you run for it, I'll shoot you with your own gun.'

Ken's one open eye was bloodshot, and he was frightened. Dawlish pushed him out of the shop. Mrs. Bray stood watching, from the counter, a tin in each hand; she hadn't touched the money. Dawlish pressed the gun into Ken's side, and they walked through the rain.

The door of number 41 was closed.

'Open it,' he ordered Ken.

The man took out a key, and unlocked the door. Dawlish pushed him inside. Gloom and dankness met him. Every door in sight was open, and there was a piece of torn paper on the stairs, another at the foot of them; a paper trail: they'd taken all the documents away, or else destroyed them.

There was a cupboard under the stairs, filled with suit-cases, wooden boxes, some flower-pots, dozens of oddments; the musty smell was revolting. Dawlish pushed Ken inside, saw that he had room to sit down, then turned the lock on him and put a chair against the door; if Ken managed to open it, he'd knock the chair over and so give warning.

Dawlish went up to the sitting-room.

The photographs were gone; the books and the papers also. Every drawer of the desk had been emptied. A few screwed-up pieces of paper lay on the carpet. He went through the rest of the silent house, and found nothing.

Kate and Martson wouldn't do a deal now, unless he could find a way to conciliate them.

He must find a way. His hand was aching badly. The flesh above and below the bandage was red and puffy; the wound wanted dressing again.

He had another look round the house, and found nothing.

He scanned the odd pieces of paper; there was nothing which might help him or the police.

He smiled grimly. What would Allen of Haslemere say to what had happened this morning? Or Trivett, of the Yard, who was long-suffering, friendly—in fact, a friend. The C.I.D. Superintendent wouldn't be able to laugh this off.

But Mick Ryan had come to see Dawlish; and had died at his gate.

He went downstairs, took the chair away, and unlocked the cupboard under the stairs, deciding to take Ken with him to Tim Jeremy's flat.

Ken wasn't there.

CHAPTER XIV

THE HOUSE NEXT DOOR

He crouched down and peered inside. A door led from this cupboard to one in the adjoining house. Some of the cases had hidden it. He opened the door, had to bend almost double in order to get into the passage next door.

It was almost identical with the one he had just left, except that it had been newly decorated.

Dawlish nursed the gun in his pocket, and went through it from top to bottom. The top floor was unfurnished and undecorated, a filthy attic. The other floors were in sharp contrast, and one bedroom was tastefully furnished and held a faint smell of perfume—*Lida*. So Kate used this room.

He found no papers.

He went down to the hall, and out by the front door. The rain still hissed gently on the streaming pavement. He walked towards the shop.

At number 37, curtains moved. Eyes were following him.

He didn't quicken his pace. As he drew near the shop, he saw Mrs. Bray rebuilding one of the towers of tins. She averted her gaze quickly. He crossed the road, knowing that he was still being watched.

He turned a corner into another drab, mean street. A man stood inside the doorway of a newspaper shop, his hands buried deep in his pockets, his chin nestling inside the upturned collar of his coat.

He fought against a temptation to glance over his shoulder, resisted it, but lengthened his stride. He reached the next corner safely, and looked round. The man was walking in his wake, a drenched figure against the drab background.

Water streamed off Dawlish's hair and soaked through his clothes.

He saw a red bus pass the end of this street.

He started to cross the road. A small car to the left was moving slowly—and suddenly he heard its engine roar as it leapt forward.

Now he knew what they were going to do.

The car came like a rocket, swift, sinister, its engine howling; and he was only half-way across the road. It wasn't five yards away from him. He didn't see the driver. He leapt desperately, and out of the corner of his eyes saw the car swing towards him. He landed on the edge of the pavement and swayed back. The car was only a yard away, with one wheel on the kerb. He flung himself forward, slipped, slithered on the greasy pavement, heard the crash as the car hit the wall of the corner house. Then something fell, heavily on to the back of his legs, pinning him down.

He'd had it; there was no escape. No hope at all. He couldn't move, and the driver of the car would finish him off.

'Oi!' A man called.

Then a whistle sounded, shrill, piercing, a lovely sound, for it was a police-whistle. There were heavy footsteps as the policeman ran up. The driver struck at Dawlish, desperately, hurriedly. The weapon caught him painfully on the back of the head, just above the neck, but without much force behind the blow.

The iron piping dropped and rang loudly on the pavement; the man turned and fled. The policeman's feet came in sight, heavy boots thumped on the pavement. He heard the man call out: 'Look after *him*!' Then he became aware of someone else, bending over him. It was a postman, wearing a cape which shone blackly and dripped rain.

'You okay, chum?'

'I'm fine,' said Dawlish. His head ached, that was all. 'You might—you might see if you can free my legs.'

'Sorry, chum. Caught you proper, they 'ave.'

Fear sprang up in Dawlish.

'How—bad?'

'Bad? Well, I dunno. Got the car right on top of yer. I don't see no blood.' He sniffed. 'What was he playing at? No use running away, when his car's smashed up; they'll trace it.'

The rain beat down, drenching him. The postman crouched down and spread out the cape, though it didn't shelter Dawlish very much. It seemed an age before others arrived. The first were two or three people from nearby houses.

A bell began to ring, and grew louder. 'Ambulance,' said a woman. Now there was a little bedraggled crowd pressing round him. Two or three cars and several cyclists had stopped. Two policemen had arrived. One of them bent over him perfunctorily, told him he was all right, and straightened up.

The note of a powerful engine was added to the clanging of the bell. Ambulance? No, this was a fire-engine.

A shriller ringing sound told him that both had arrived.

Then came a doctor, short, squat, bluff—complete with black

bag. He bent down. 'Now, what's all this about? Where does it hurt most?'

'It doesn't,' said Dawlish.

'Oh, that's good. Probably you'll be lucky, can't tell until we've got that car off your legs. It won't be long, now. If you'd like a shot of morphia—'

'No!' Dawlish felt the word explode inside him, then grinned sheepishly. 'Thanks.'

The pressure on his legs was greater now; not actually painful, but heavy and persistent. The numbness and the fact that he was imprisoned there was the worst part about it all. He kept quite still, not even moving his head and arms.

The crowd moved away reluctantly; there were more policemen than Dawlish had realised; this was really a sensation.

'Ready?' a man called in a stentorian voice.

A police-sergeant bent over Dawlish.

'Just going to lift the car, they are. I—*strewth*! You're—Mr. *Daw*lish.'

There were creaking, groaning, rending sounds—and the weight eased; more than eased, it disappeared. Dawlish raised his head and squinted round.

A dozen men stood about the saloon car, all had big iron bars which had been thrust beneath the car. The car was inches above his legs.

'Lift—now again, *lift*!'

There was no weight at all on Dawlish's legs, but the car was still above them, and if it slipped—there wouldn't be much hope for him. '*Lift!*' Dawlish felt his forehead warm and sticky; he was wet, not only with the rain but with perspiration. Two men were crouching by his legs, why didn't they pull him out? Suddenly three policemen appeared by Dawlish's side, pulled gently but firmly at his shoulders, and soon had him clear of the car.

*   *   *

'That's what I call luck,' said the doctor, smiling broadly as he looked down at Dawlish's bare legs. 'Nothing but bruises. No bones broken. You'll have to take it easy for a day or two, that's all.'

It wasn't any use pretending; he couldn't walk with any comfort. His left leg was more painful than his right.

A car drew up.

'Take it easy, we'll help you up.' Two constables took his arms and raised him to his feet. They half-carried him to the big car. He climbed in, without much discomfort, and sank back gratefully. 'Flat 3, 21a Jermyn Street, that's it, isn't it, Mr. Dawlish?'

He'd given them Tim Jeremy's address.

'Thanks, yes.'

The car moved off, sleek and smooth-running, and he closed his eyes and drew at a cigarette. He was warm; his legs ached, his head was light, but that was all. His hand was most painful.

He'd have to tell the police something; he would have to decide how much, if anything, to keep to himself. The theme of his thoughts remained unchanged; could he still persuade Kate and Martson that he would do a deal? He knew so much that was important. At a word from him, the police could put out a call for Steen, Martson, Kate, Ken, and Mulligan. Ought he to withhold the information?

Here! This wasn't Jermyn Street, this was—the Embankment! That big white building on the right was Scotland Yard, the C.I.D. Division. Confound their knavish tricks, they had brought him to the Yard!

He sat up as the car turned into the gates, and came to a standstill outside the entrance of the New Building, which overlooked the Thames.

As it stopped, Superintendent Trivett came down the steps.

Trivett, tall, dressed in dark blue and a credit to his tailor, wore his Homburg hat on the back of his head and showed his dark hair. He grinned as he approached the car and opened the door. He was a handsome, lean man who might be taken at a glance for somebody in the City.

'Curses on the heads of all policemen,' growled Dawlish.

'I thought you'd think that. But I don't like the idea that someone is running around trying to bump you off. Move over—I'm coming to the flat with you.'

CHAPTER XV

THE VIEW OF SCOTLAND YARD

'I want to avoid Tim's flat.' said Dawlish.

'Why?'

'Because someone I don't want you to see is waiting for me there.'

'Oh,' said Trivett. He took the cigarette from his lips. 'Where else would you like to go?'

'My club. I've a spare suit there. There's also a lift, near the front door; I needn't scandalise the corpses.'

'All right,' said Trivett.

So the first skirmish was won. Trivett's appearance having forced the issue, Dawlish had to decide very quickly just how much to confide. It wouldn't be any use beating about the bush. Trivett knew about Mick Ryan's death, guessed why he was in London.

They pulled up outside the club.

Trivett sat by the window, overlooking the Mall and the wet greenery of St. James's Park, in a large and comfortable arm-chair in Dawlish's usual room. He was smiling as if feeling benevolent.

'This is the Ryan case, isn't it? That car tried to run you down, and the driver tried to finish you off with a piece of iron piping.'

'Yes. Did your boys get the driver, by any chance?'

'No.'

'And then you wonder why I have no faith in policemen!'

'Pat, when are you going to grow up? It isn't the kind of thing you can handle on your own. But,' said Trivett gently, 'you might be able to lend us a hand. Might, I said. That's the official view of Scotland Yard, old chap.'

'Well, Bill,' said Dawlish, heavily.

'I suppose one of the reasons why you thought you could handle this better on your own was that the girl told you that Ryan had been to the Yard, and we cold-shouldered him. But we had our reasons, Patrick.'

'Hmm,' said Dawlish, and sipped more beer. 'Yes, I suppose so. When you gave Ryan the brush-off it was a tactical manœuvre; actually you already knew something about the job, and were going your own way about it. And that way was *very* successful. Ryan was murdered in cold blood, for a start. Why wasn't he followed?'

'He was.'

'Then why wasn't he saved?'

Trivett said: 'Pat, don't take that line. There's one type of man you can never protect properly—the man who wants to give you the slip. It was the same with Helen Graves, except that we did get as far as Dorking after her. She booked to Dorking, to put us off the scent. Our man wasn't so good, got off, and didn't realise in time that she stayed on the train.'

'All small saloon cars were stopped on the road from Haslemere on the night of Ryan's death. Numbers were taken, passengers and drivers were questioned. They were all able to answer satisfactorily. But one of the stopped cars was the one which got you an hour ago.'

'How was the driver able to give a satisfactory answer if he'd just come from killing Ryan?'

'Obviously what happened was that the murderers changed cars, not far from your place, and they were only looking for small saloons, you know. This car was driven by a woman; there were no passengers. Now, Pat, how much do you know about Lord Calder?'

Dawlish went through the whole story, finding Trivett more than normally attentive. Through the open window the chimes of Big Ben came clearly; it was noon. Dawlish had talked for nearly half an hour. Finally, he said: 'I didn't enjoy that walk from number 41, Bill. I had a feeling that they wouldn't let me alone. But the car trick caught me.'

'And are you still anxious to avenge Mick Ryan?'

'That's one way of putting it.'

'What does Felicity think about all this?'

'She'll know that it must go on.'

'Hmm,' murmured Trivett. 'It's a very big and very bad business. The little trick about the photographs, for instance. Very cunning. But—it suggests these people could really use your help?'

Dawlish said: 'My mind did work a little, this morning, you know. I thought at first that the whole thing was a washout, as far as doing a deal with them was concerned, but there's still a chance. For instance, the police needn't visit Killiger Street. Or have you been there already.'

'No. I held off until I saw you.'

'Thanks. Kate and Martson might assume that I haven't told you, so I might become a prospect again. That's one reason why I didn't want you to go to Tim's place.'

'Who's there?'

'Helen Graves—I hope,' exclaimed Dawlish. He turned abruptly and grabbed the telephone. 'Give me Mayfair 21213,' he said urgently. Trivett leaned forward in his chair, as anxious as Dawlish.

'Tim?'

'Hallo, Pat! How long are you going to be? I like entertaining lovelies, but this one—'

'So she's there?'

'Oh, yes. Been here for an hour. When are you coming?'

'As soon as I can. Don't let her go. Play tiddlywinks or tell her your life story.'

'I have,' said Tim sadly. 'She's more interested in yours.'

'I'll be seeing you,' said Dawlish.

'So Helen Graves is there all right,' Trivett said.

'Yes. I'd like to send her away somewhere quite safe. Can do?'

'I don't see why not,' said Trivett.

'Another hopeful thing,' said Dawlish, 'is that she doesn't believe I'm going to consult the police. She thinks I'm in this for what I can get out of it. Cunning Kate might ask her a question or two, and—'

'But you're going to send her away, so Kate can't.'

'Better she doesn't know I'm mixed up with you, all the same,' said Dawlish. 'Bill—how much do *you* know about Lord Jeremiah Calder? What made you give Ryan the brush-off? What's the game? Do you really think that I can help?'

'Before Ryan turned up at your place, I'd been wondering if I dared brave Felicity's wrath, and ask you to lend a hand. It's your kind of job. I needn't take much time telling you about it, either— the details will be filled in as they crop up. Briefly, then—'

He sounded casual, almost nonchalant, but there was a note of gravity in all he said as well as in his expression.

'Calder appears to be having a rough time, Pat. Whether he's being blackmailed or not, I don't know. But he's shut himself up, hired bodyguards, and generally behaves as if he needs police protection and daren't ask for it. I've only one lead—a woman. Judging from your vivid descriptions—Kate!'

Dawlish said: 'Could it be simple, Bill? Kate got him by the short hairs, compromised him as she's compromised me, and then put on the black?'

'I think that's part of it.'

'Could be she wants his keys and entry to the strong room, but he's gone on strike?'

'There's something else.' Trivett was emphatic.

'What is it?'

'I can't tell you.'

Dawlish looked at him thoughtfully.

'All right, you can't,' Dawlish said. 'I won't complain about that. You're not sure what it is, you must find out, and you'd like me to act as Aunt Sally?'

Trivett said: 'That's it, and no one must know, Pat. Not even Felicity. Certainly not Tim. You won't be alone, of course, we'll be working where we can. But I can't tell you what else we're doing.'

Dawlish hardly hesitated.

'Call it a deal.'

'Thanks, Pat,' said Bill Trivett.

It took Dawlish a long time to get dressed. He wanted to see Helen and talk to Tim very much indeed, yet he also needed his hand dressed. So he sent for a doctor whom he knew. The doctor arrived just after one forty-five, stripped the dressing off the wound, and revealed a congealed, raw, ugly mess.

* * *

He heard the bell ring inside the flat. Then tall, lean, solemn Tim Jeremy opened the door.

'You've been long enough,' he growled.

'Sorry,' said Dawlish.

'Anyone would think you'd been pushed under a bus,' complained Tim, then noticed the new white bandage.

'Sorry,' repeated Dawlish. He moved forward gingerly, like a cripple.

'Here!' exclaimed Tim. 'What's this? Senile decay?'

'Knocked about a bit, but no bones broken. Sorry Helen's been such a wet blanket.'

Tim helped him to hobble inside.

Tim laughed; it sounded hollow. Dawlish had a feeling that all was not well with him.

'Don't be an ass,' he said. 'She's—well, you ought to know, I gather you're good friends.' There was tartness in Tim's voice.

Dawlish exclaimed: '*What?*' He stared at Tim, wondering if Tim had seen one of those photographs; if so, it would explain Tim's mood.

Then a door opened, and Kate stood smiling at him.

CHAPTER XVI

KIND KATE

'Hallo, Pat,' she said.

He hadn't really noticed the warmth of her voice before. It wasn't just warmth, either; it had another quality. She spoke as if he were the only man in the world.

'I do hope you weren't badly hurt.'

'Hurt?' echoed Dawlish.

Her eyes became more violet than blue, and there was a great depth of humour in them.

'Your hand—you have hurt it, haven't you?'

'Oh, that. Yes. It's all right. Which reminds me, I want a scarf for a sling.' He hobbled, on his own, towards the door. Kate didn't back away, but took his right arm and pressed it closely to her. She helped him, with easy strength, to an upright chair.

'You'll be more comfortable in that,' she said.

Dawlish said slowly: 'Where's Helen?'

'We're looking after Helen. We waylaid her taxi. Your friend Bert didn't like it, but he couldn't do anything about it!'

'Your second mistake,' Dawlish said. 'You shouldn't have taken her away, Kate.'

'But she's such a good bargaining weapon. She was with poor Mick, and now she is with you.' She sat on the arm of a chair, smelling of *Lida*, looking as if her middle name ought to be *Allure*, and opened her handbag, producing a small gold cigarette-case.

There was warm intimacy in the air. Tim looked strained, worried—almost distressed. He was not a man who could easily hide his feelings; and he was fond of Felicity.

'You shouldn't have kept Tim away from me for so long,' said Kate, and her voice was like syrup. 'It's not fair, darling. I think he's great fun.'

'Am I in the way?' asked Tim. His voice was hoarse, and he looked past Dawlish towards the window. He was a modern man; a cynic; he had few illusions, but he believed that Pat and Felicity Dawlish were the happiest married couple on God's earth.

He went out of the room.

The front door slammed.

Kate laughed.

'How do you like the boomerang, darling?'

'We seem to be convincing the world that we're old friends.'

She was still close to him. He didn't like the look in her eyes. The violet-blue depths clouded, as if with smoke; and there was a hint of fire, half-hidden by the cloud.

'You killed Steen.'

'Let's say he committed suicide.'

'What a comfortable conscience! You throw a man down-stairs, using that brute strength of yours on a weakling, you break his back and he dies in terrible agony—'

'Steen knew the stakes,' said Dawlish. 'You may lose, too. I might. Don't talk morals to me, my pretty.' He fingered his cigarette-case slowly, pressing his big fingers against the silver. 'Did you send that car?'

'Ken did. He's known Steen a long time. Whatever you do, be careful of Ken.'

Not a muscle of Dawlish's face moved.

'I think you can work with us,' said Kate. 'Perhaps it's a good thing that Steen's gone. You and he would never have got along well. You and I can. You and Martson can.'

'Fifty-fifty,' said Dawlish.

'Now Steen's gone, you might get Martson up to a third.'

Dawlish said sharply: 'I'm not haggling. I've told you my terms, and they're final. This is big money.'

He didn't know for sure that it was big money; he wanted her to believe that he knew more than she had thought.

'What have you got to offer for your share?'

'A quiescent police force, where you're concerned.'

'Go on.'

'Isn't that enough? The police are after Ryan's murderer. He went to see them—did you know that?'

'They wouldn't listen to him, he hadn't anything much to say. Just that Calder was harassed.'

Dawlish said: 'They knew Ryan was right.'

Not a feature of her face moved; she was like a statue—a figure of unsurpassable beauty.

'How do you know that?' she asked softly.

'The police told me?'

'When?'

'When they first asked me to help them over the Calder business,' said Dawlish.

'You're lying,' she said.

'Oh, no. Trivett is handling this job, and Trivett is no fool, Kate. He's had a go at me this morning. He wanted to know where I'd been and all about it. I convinced him that I didn't know, said I'd been shanghaied, woke up, found myself with

Helen in a room, and got away from the house. I told him I'd sent Helen away in a taxi, stayed to look round, and got myself run over. I added that I'd two legs that wouldn't work and a hand which will have to be amputated if I'm not careful, and I've had quite enough of this lousy business. But he won't accept that attitude for long. He'll give me a few days, then be after me to help again. He thinks I know something. When he comes again, I can tell him the truth—or a few highly coloured lies. I think it's worth fifty-fifty. Go and tell Martson so.'

Kate said softly: 'All this might be a frame-up, Dawlish. I think perhaps you'd be better dead. If you can't talk, they can't get me or Martson.'

'Perhaps you're right. But I like to be different from other men, and I've arranged to talk after death. I've named you, Martson, Steen, Ken, and Mulligan. I've left a letter where it will be opened after my death. The obvious things have to be done sometimes, you know.'

That took her by surprise, but she hid it cleverly.

'I'll talk to Martson,' she promised, and went towards the door. She was in the hall when he called out:

'Kate. Come back.'

She faced him, from the threshold.

'Remember why I threw Steen down the stairs? He wouldn't play the game my way. The first condition to working together is Helen's release. I want her here in two hours' time. If she doesn't come—no deal, and you'll be driven underground.'

Tim Jeremy came back an hour after Kate had gone; he was not drunk, but was undoubtedly squiffy. He lounged across the room towards Dawlish, who was sitting now in an easy chair. Throbbing legs, throbbing hand, and bursting head; he was in no mood to face a doubting Timothy. But Tim, being Tim, would force an issue.

'I am not,' announced Tim, 'a prude. But I must have had Victorian forebears, or a Puritan ancestor.'

Dawlish screwed up his eyes and forced his shrieking nerves to be calm about this. Because—he had to convince Tim that his, Tim's, conclusions were right; if he were to work 'with' Kate, it must be a secret between him and the police. No one else must know—yet. *Not even Felicity.*

Tim was very serious; not pretending, in dead earnest. That puzzled Dawlish. He had expected a few tart words and then tolerance; he hadn't expected this or anything like this. And his aching muscles and taut nerves protested; that was why his voice was low and even.

'I don't follow, old chap.'

'I was talking of my ancestry. And the curious notion that some things are not done. Especially by—you. Damn it, Pat, you ought to know how I feel.'

Tim took out a cigarette; wasn't satisfied with it, went to a cabinet and got some whisky. He poured out more than a stiffener, and tossed it down.

'Look here, Pat.' He was exerting himself to be calm, just as Dawlish was. 'I can stand nonsense from most people, but—not from you. I'm in love with Felicity. I won't stand by and watch you—'

The jarring nerves and sinews, the protesting muscles, the throbbing hand, all seemed to scream at one and the same time, and then to explode inside Dawlish.

He kept silent; he couldn't have spoken then, whatever Tim said or wanted to hear. He had known Tim as a fast friend; trusty, loyal, ready to plunge into such affairs as this with a blind faith in his leadership. A man to take for granted. A man even to pity, sometimes, because he was for ever in and out of love; or in and out of *affaires*; twice engaged, twice breaking it off.

He didn't trust himself to be tied to one woman; or so Dawlish had thought. Instead, he was in love with Felicity; and he had to choose this moment to say so.

Dawlish opened his eyes and found Tim looking at him, flushed, ready for anything—abuse, protests—anything. But Tim's face was going round and round; so was the ceiling, the floor, the furniture.

'Well, what are you going to do about it?' Tim asked.

Dawlish said: 'Help me to the bedroom. Get a nurse in. Sorry, Tim. Sorry about everything.'

Of course, Tim didn't get a nurse, but set to work. He was much more himself when Dawlish was in bed—his, Tim's bed, not the tiny one in the spare room. He discovered, moreover, that Dawlish hadn't had lunch, so he prepared a light meal. He was solicitous, and yet not quite himself. A barrier made of shadow had grown between them, and Dawlish couldn't pierce it. It was like a clinging mist.

He closed his eyes, and dozed; he felt more rested, and less raw. The sun was shining weakly through a corner of the window. The murmur of traffic was constantly in his ears. Tim wasn't in the room now, was probably doing something in the flat.

He heard a ring at the front-door bell, and it jarred through his head. Tim answered, and there was a murmured conversation. Then something tore; paper; Tim uttered a strange sound, like a groan.

The door burst open and Tim came in, eyes ablaze, cheeks flaming, holding something in his hand. He strode to the bed and flung the something at Dawlish; a piece of white paper. It was more than paper; the corner caught Dawlish on the cheek, and hurt. It was cardboard. He groped for it. Tim snatched it and held it a few inches from his eyes.

It was the photograph; a print of the one that Kate had shown him that morning. He didn't think beyond Kate, and hatred for her; he knew how Steen had felt, now. He was hardly aware of the passion in Tim's eyes, the disgust, the loathing.

He didn't trust himself to speak, in case he said the wrong thing. Whatever decision he made now would probably be a wrong one.

Tim dropped the photograph and stood back from the bed.

'Nice chap,' he said. 'Everything Felicity ever wanted. For years I've told myself that I'm glad she married you, not me. You'll have to get out of here.'

'Oh, shut up,' gasped Dawlish—and then, surprising himself, he began to laugh. It wasn't with amusement, it wasn't because he wanted to laugh or really saw the funny side of anything; it was not far from hysteria. The blow on the head, probably—he had concussion. Whatever it was, he laughed, although he knew that Tim felt like hitting him. Tim stood only a yard from the bed, with the photograph in his hand and an unfamiliar, bleak expression on his face.

Dawlish managed to check his laughter, ached all over, and felt more light-headed; it *must* be the blow over the head, it couldn't be anything else. A drug? He'd smoked Kate's cigarette.

'And I suppose you ought to be sent home, to her,' said Tim.

'Keep her out of this,' he said.

'Make it nice and easy for you,' said Tim. 'Oh, no. I'll ring her.'

There was a telephone by the side of the bed. He picked it up, and began to dial, but before he'd finished there was another ring at the front-door bell. 'Damnation!' he muttered, and banged the receiver down. He went out, without looking at Dawlish.

The front door opened.

A woman spoke, and there was a pause: then Tim said:

'*Clear out.*'

'But—' the woman began.

'Tim!' called Dawlish. He sat up, and his head swam. He pushed the bedclothes back. 'Tim, hold on!' He managed to get out of bed. The door was open. He reached it, leaning heavily against the side. Tim stood in the doorway leading to the landing, and Helen stood outside.

'I've told you,' Tim said, softly.

'Tim! Don't be a fool!'

Tim swung round, eyes blazing again. 'Shut up! If you think you're going to use my flat for your brothel, you're making a hell of a mistake. If you want to be with her, go with her, but she isn't going to stay here for thirty seconds.'

Helen backed away in fright.

Then someone else reached the landing, someone who must have heard all that Tim said. They were light, familiar footsteps. Dawlish wasn't surprised when he saw Felicity take Helen's arm, and heard her speak in a quiet, reasoning voice.

'What's all this about, Tim?'

Tim didn't say anything, but backed away. Felicity still held Helen's arm, and brought her into the flat. Felicity closed the door, and then looked across to the bedroom, and saw Dawlish.

CHAPTER XVII

FELICITY

Dawlish tried to smile at her, was foolish enough to let go of the door-post, and nearly fell. Felicity hurried, and took his weight.

'Help me, Tim,' she commanded.

Tim made a curious noise in his throat, but didn't move. Felicity put her shoulder against Dawlish's chest, and helped him back to the bed. She smoothed out the bedclothes as he leaned against her, and turned up the photograph. It lay face uppermost, with its silent, lying message, and Felicity's strength seemed to ooze away.

Tim was now in the room.

'I'm sorry, Fel,' he said.

Felicity looked at him, past him—and then at Dawlish. She didn't smile; her eyes were dazed. She pushed the bedclothes farther back, and the photograph moved with them.

'Help me with him,' she said.

She didn't sound like Felicity at all, any more than Tim had sounded like Tim. Dawlish felt petulant; angry; petulant again. He wished he could refuse to be put to bed, but he hadn't the strength.

'Have you sent for a doctor?' Felicity asked in that strange, unfamiliar voice.

'No. Fel, I'm terribly sorry. If I'd known you were on the stairs, I wouldn't—'

'Call a doctor,' said Felicity. 'Helen, go into the drawing-room and sit down, you look tired out.'

Dawlish was left alone in the room, and heard Tim talking on the telephone in the hall. Dawlish didn't want a doctor, but—'

It was hard to convince himself that the main thing had gone right. Helen was here.

Kate had accepted the condition, and wanted him to play. Trivett's face hovered in his mind's eye, the grim and sombre Trivett who had leaned forward and said impressively: 'No one must know, Pat. *Not even Felicity.* Certainly not Tim. There might be difficulties, but—that's essential.' Dawlish had said: 'Done,' as simply as that.

He dozed off, not really asleep or unconscious but only vaguely aware of where he was. The weight which had been so heavy on his legs now seemed to be on his chest, a physical thing, pressing him down heavily.

It was the doctor who'd seen him at the Club. He didn't say much to Tim or Felicity while he inspected Dawlish, found the bump on his head, and smiled secretly, as if he now knew the root of the trouble. He filled a hypodermic syringe, and Felicity turned up Dawlish's sleeve. The doctor rubbed the inside of the elbow with spirit, and then put in the needle and pressed the plunger. Dawlish was just aware of the prick.

He felt all right. He was hungry. That annoyed him, because it was dark and he sensed that it was the middle of the night. He also sensed that he was in an unfamiliar room; certainly not at *Four Ways*. He'd woken up recently with something like the same feeling as he had now, even to the hunger.

Then he remembered Helen.

He was dreaming. This was exactly the same as when he'd woken at Killiger Street. He was at Tim's flat.

A foot brushed against his.

He eased himself up, stretched out gingerly for the table lamp, and tried to stop his heart from thumping. His head didn't ache, that was something; his legs were tender even beneath the light weight of the bedclothes. He pushed the lamp against the wall, caught his breath, in case it had disturbed whoever was next to him, and then found the switch.

A soft light came on.

He turned—and found Felicity looking at him, her eyes dark and cloudy with sleep.

He left the light on, and relaxed. Felicity didn't move, but he knew she was still looking at him. He found it difficult to frame words; Trivett's warning and the importance the C.I.D. attached to it jostled in his mind with the need for saying something—anything reassuring—to Felicity.

'How are you feeling, Pat?' asked Felicity in a low-pitched voice.

'Better. Much better.'

'That's good.' She eased herself up on her elbow, to see the time. 'It's half-past four. You've slept the clock round.'

'Drugged sleep,' said Dawlish. 'How's Tim? Finding Tim in deadly earnest is a revelation.'

It came to him that even though Tim had never uttered a word, Felicity must have known all about it for some time.

'Tim's often earnest, you just haven't noticed it,' said Felicity. 'Helen's still here. Is she still in danger?'

'Not at the moment. She might be, if anything goes wrong

with the great plan. Fel.' He touched her arm. 'This is going to be one of the stickiest shows we've ever touched. A lot of things that seem true, aren't. It's deep, complicated, and dangerous, and I've got to see it through.'

'Yes, of course,' said Felicity.

Dawlish said: 'And photographs can lie.'

She winced, as if he'd struck her; he thought she was going to break down; tears actually swam in her eyes. But she forced them back, and then said quietly:

'Hadn't you better get the job done first, and sort other things out later?'

She'd spoken rather like that, although with less intensity, when they'd talked at *Four Ways*.

'What are you going to do next?' asked Felicity.

'Get properly on my feet again,' said Dawlish. 'Then start coping with Kate. Have you heard about Kate?'

'Yes.'

'And I'd like Helen to go away to some quiet little spot where Kate and her friends can't get at her.'

'Perhaps you've a week-end cottage somewhere,' said Felicity.

He knew that the moment the words were out she regretted them. He knew, then, that trying to smooth things out now would help neither of them.

He said: 'No, Fel, I haven't one, but I think Helen ought to go out of London and I think I ought to stay here. Will you look after Helen?'

She hesitated for a long time. Then: 'Yes.'

'I should think *Four Ways* would be best,' said Dawlish. 'I'll make sure that you're protected down there. I don't exactly expect trouble, but it might come. Like Tim to be down with you?'

'No. Tim will want to stay up here and help you. He wouldn't be happy if he left you to fend for yourself, whatever he says now. Have you discovered what the trouble is all about?'

'No,' said Dawlish.

They lay awake until dawn began to spread gently across the sky. The song of the sparrows near by was a pitiful echo of the bird-song at *Four Ways*.

Felicity and Helen had left for *Four Ways*.

No word had come from Kate or Steen or Martson, but there was a small paragraph in most of the newspapers, saying that the body of a man, who had died of a broken back, had been found in the Thames, near Shadwell. Trivett telephoned, to say that he would send messages in future, because he thought it possible that the 'others' would manage to tap the telephone to the flat. He asked Dawlish to send messages, and only to telephone the Yard in an emergency. If Dawlish wanted any special things done to help him he had only to say so. And:

'We're counting on you. We've got to get to the bottom of this. I've seen Tim, and—'

'He *talked*?'

'He gave me an idea of your difficulties, and I'm not really surprised. I've seen that photograph. Don't tell Felicity what you're doing, will you?'

'I won't,' said Dawlish slowly.

Tim didn't refer to what had happened the previous afternoon. He came to Dawlish and asked for orders.

Dawlish tried to be natural. 'Later,' he said. 'Heard anything from Ted?'

After he left Piccadilly last night, following Helen Graves, he was involved in an accident. Not serious, but he had a nasty bump over the head, needing a couple of stitches. He's out for a bit, I'm afraid. That leaves just the two of us. How far is Trivett helping?'

Dawlish said: 'Better assume that we're on our own.'

On the second day, telephone engineers called at the flat below, and only Dawlish suspected their real purpose. He didn't try to investigate, but had no doubt that a wire had been fitted to tap all calls from Tim's flat.

For three days there was a period of unnatural calm. Dawlish telephoned Felicity each day, but everything was on the surface.

No word came from Kate or Martson, and no further word came from Trivett.

Dawlish even found himself wondering whether Kate and Martson had decided not to play. But he still had the genuine keys safe at the safe deposit. The time would come when they would have to try to get them from him.

On the afternoon of the fourth day he left the flat. He could walk fairly well, and his arm was comfortable in its sling. In another forty-eight hours, he would be almost as fit as ever.

He walked towards Green Park and across it. The day was fine, there was a crispness which made champagne of the air and brought a sparkle to eyes, freshness to trees not yet touched with autumn's colours. He dawdled, deliberately, to find out whether he was followed, but noticed no one taking any particular interest in him.

He reached St. James's Park, strolled across the Horse Guards' Parade and out into Whitehall. At Trafalgar Square he began to look round for a taxi. A newsvendor shouted his wares raucously, and Dawlish bought a paper, with half an eye on the road for a free taxi. One hove in sight. Dawlish shot up his hand, the taxi stopped, and he sank back, pleasantly relaxed.

He opened the *Evening Cry*. Splashed across the front page was a headline which didn't at first convey much to him.

MILLIONAIRE'S HOME BURGLED

Thieves' Poor Haul—Footman Injured

Thieves broke into the home of Lord Calder, millionaire financier, in the early hours of this morning. Arthur Morton, footman at the house, interrupted the thieves and was injured when he attempted to stop them. The thieves failed to break into the strong-room, and their haul was small—

Dawlish didn't read on.

The lull was over. Kate and Martson now knew that he still had the real keys. This was exactly what he wanted—something to get his teeth into. It would help him not to brood over personal worries.

A glistening green car passed the taxi; Kate was at the wheel.

CHAPTER XVIII

FIFTY-FIFTY

She smiled and waved to him, went ahead and slowed down, drawing into the kerb. He tapped on the window of the cab, and the driver leaned back.

'Put me down here, please.'

'Okay.'

Her beauty made his heart miss a beat when he went towards her. She touched the seat next to her.

Dawlish went round to the other side, and climbed in.

'Going to take me for a ride?'

'Haven't you taken us for one?'

'I don't get you.'

'Neither of us gave the keys a thought,' she said, and laughed infectiously. 'Where are the real keys?'

'Waiting for me when I want to use them.'

She let in the clutch and the car moved off. She drove along Piccadilly, swung round the wide approach to Constitution Hill opposite St. George's Hospital, passed through the gateway and pulled into the kerb.

'Still fifty-fifty?'

'Yes.'

'You've made Martson hate you, but I think he'll agree.' She took off her gloves and rested her hand on Dawlish's, lightly, almost caressingly. 'You'll have to be very careful of Martson,' she said.

'As of Ken.'

'Martson much more than Ken. Pat, I didn't realise you had a good mind. I thought you were just a hulking great brute who battered his way to what he wanted. I'm sorry. *Have* you the keys?'

'Oh yes, I took them from Ryan.'

'We must get into Calder's strong room; it's vital.'

'You've made it very simple,' said Dawlish dryly. 'He'll double his private guards, may have the locks changed, and probably ask for police protection.'

'Oh, no,' said Kate confidently, 'he won't have the police. He won't have the locks changed, either. Young Ryan was smart. He had a set made, and replaced the originals. As for the police, they'll nose about for a while, but he'll soon send them away. You're not afraid of his private guards, are you?'

'I wouldn't know.'

'If you're going to have a fifty-fifty cut, you'll have to work for it,' said Kate. 'We have to get into Calder's strong room this week. I don't think you'd like to trust anyone else with the keys, would you? You'll have to do it yourself. Can you do it to-night?'

'No, and nothing will persuade me. It's Wednesday. I might go on Friday. Before I go, I'll have to know what I'm looking for.'

'You won't,' said Kate. 'We'll trust you with some things but not that, darling.'

She smiled into his face—as if he meant the world to her.

'Just you and me?' said Dawlish.

'How quick you are! Yes, just you and me. You know, Pat, you and I could go places.'

'I suppose we'd make a good pair,' conceded Dawlish. 'But supposing we stick to business? I haven't committed myself to an emotional entanglement.'

'Why must it be emotional?' she asked, and touched his hand again. 'Pat—' The word was a sigh. 'Do you know what's in Calder's strong room?'

'I know that when this is over it will mean big money, and I want big money, but there's no point in pretending I know many details. Certainly not about Calder. Neither Ryan nor Helen knew why you wanted to rob him. What is in the strong room?'

'I don't know, either,' said Kate.

For a moment, he almost believed her.

Why had she said that? Was this a move as deep and cunning as the fathomless pit of her mind.

'I once told you that Martson was clever. He won't tell me, and he certainly won't tell you.'

'That sounds wonderful. We go hand in hand to Calder's house, break through his bodyguards, use the keys for which at least one man has died, get into the strong room—and then, presumably, telephone Martson and ask him what it is he wants.'

'He'll tell us what it looks like.'

'I can't tell one jewel from another.'

'Oh, not *jewels*,' said Kate, and laughed. 'It's something easily recognisable. Documents of some kind, but I don't know what they're about. They're worth—Martson says they're worth—more money than Calder has. He's supposed to be the seventh richest man in England, isn't he?'

'All right, we go in and get them. Then we hand them over to Martson, who says thanks very much, and shuts the door on us.'

'No, he won't do that,' said Kate. 'I want my share, too. I think

I'm more likely to get it from you than Martson.' She laughed again, and although it was a lovely sound, there was something ugly about it; so much about her was contradictory. 'Darling, we get the documents, and before we take them to Martson, we find out what they are. That's the only sensible thing to do. Then we shall really have a hold over him.'

'No double-cross,' murmured Dawlish.

'Not for us.'

'I don't trust you and I don't trust Martson,' said Dawlish. 'But—sad fact—I can do with money. Much money. Friday night, about one o'clock. By to-morrow I want a sketch plan of Calder's house, with all details, so that we can get in easily and not get lost.'

Kate said: 'We'll spend Friday evening together, Pat. Go gay! At my flat, if you like, it isn't far from Calder's house. And at one o'clock—'

'At one o'clock, we'll meet at your flat. I don't want to see you again until then. And we'll meet outside, and keep our minds on business, honey. Where do you live?' asked Dawlish.

She told him; and soon afterwards, drove off alone.

Dawlish sauntered towards the Mall, and went to his club, there concocting a message for Trivett. He reported both the interference with his telephone and the Friday-night assignation, and asked Trivett to arrange for him to have a front room, on the ground floor, at the corner of Wickin Lane, where Kate lived. He sent the message by a club porter.

The plans arrived by special messenger next morning. They weren't rough sketches, but proper blue-prints, perfectly executed. Three places were marked, weak spots where entry to the house could be forced. They arrived while Tim was out, and Dawlish said nothing to him. Later in the day, there also arrived a note from Trivett; he'd received Dawlish's message and would act on it. The front room of the corner house at Wickin Lane was at his disposal, and the door would be open.

Early on Friday afternoon, Tim came in unexpectedly, while Dawlish was looking at the blue-prints. He was pale and looked as if he hadn't slept well on the past few nights.

'Busy?'

'I am, rather. Plans.' Dawlish grinned.

'I wish I knew what you were playing at.'

'It's deep and dangerous. Doing anything to-night?'

'No.'

'At a quarter to one, I'd like you to be near Lord Calder's place. You know it?'

'Milton Square, yes.'

'Hide in the doorway of number 12, which is a few doors from a corner nearly opposite Calder's. I'll give you a bunch of keys before you go. About one o'clock, I'll arrive at Milton Square, and I won't be on my own. Hand me over the keys. Also, hand me a couple of little bags of ammonia—you know, the burstable bags. You may be able to come with me. If you can't, give me a couple of hours. If I don't turn up, tell Trivett exactly what we've been doing.'

Tim said slowly: 'So Trivett's in this.'

'He'll have to be if things go wrong to-night. It wouldn't surprise me if they go wrong. I don't trust any luscious lovely, much.'

'Don't you?' asked Tim stonily.

It was a perfect night, with no moon. The stars had vivid brightness, a gentle wind gave the night air a crispness which made it good to be alive.

It was midnight when Dawlish left the Jermyn Street flat and took the wheel of the Jaguar, which was parked outside. He thought that Tim watched him from the window; Tim was to leave five minutes after him. He drove slowly through the nearly deserted streets, seeing more policemen than ordinary people.

A small car had been parked along the street, not far behind him, and crawled in his wake.

He felt danger as acute as when he had left Killiger Street. Those watching eyes, the possibility of a sudden attack, of sudden death, loomed up like a shadow. Kate wanted one thing—the keys, and because he was leaving for the assignation, she would expect him to have them on his person.

She lived in a flat little more than ten minutes' walk from Milton Square. The car behind had only its sidelights, and he couldn't see the men in it; or how many men there were.

He passed Kate's flat.

She'd told him she was at the front, on the first floor, and there was a lighted window.

He switched on his headlamps. Wickin Lane was bathed with bright light, but no lurking figures showed up; all was quiet. The car hadn't turned after him. He drove past the house to a mews a little farther on, and turned the car into it. There, he switched off the headlights and sat for a few moments, pondering. His left hand was out of a sling, but it was still tender.

He got out of the car, and felt in his pockets. He had a gun—Ken's gun—several cracksman's tools, and a coil of stout cord.

The starry, silent night was lovely. There were a few lighted windows, the sound of music floated from a doorway in the mews, a dim light shone on a sign: '*The Blue Moon Club*.' He knew the place for a poky nightclub, which thrived on innocents who wanted to see night life in London.

He went to the corner and peered along the narrow street.

There were two lighted lamps, one near Kate's flat. In the light, he saw a man walking towards him, yet he'd heard no sound of footsteps. Shadows hid Dawlish as he slipped into the corner house. The door was open, the front room empty.

A clock struck the half-hour.

Would they attack him for the keys?

Another car turned into the mews, and he believed that it was the one which had followed him. It drew up on the far corner, and two men got out. He pressed close against the window. The men approached his car and peered in, as if to make sure that he wasn't still sitting in it.

The men coming along from the far end of the alley paused on the opposite corner, and one of those from the car crossed the road to join him. Dawlish distinguished a few softly spoken words. *'Seen him?' 'No.' 'He's around somewhere.' 'Hasn't he gone to see her?' 'No.' 'Cunning beggar.' 'We'll get him.'*

There were two windows, enabling Dawlish to see the mews and Wickin Lane. He couldn't have been better placed. One of the men walked along the street again, the others conferred not ten yards away from Dawlish, but he couldn't hear anything. The man who had walked off stopped near one of the lamps, just in sight.

Dawlish saw his silhouette and the movement of his arm as he threw something upwards. There was a sharp tinkle of breaking glass and the lamp went out. Dawlish became accustomed to the deeper gloom. By craning his neck, he could see the man, waiting outside Kate's house.

'Hanging around somewhere.' The voice was Ken's. 'Maybe he's gone into the *Blue Moon*. Good place to lose himself for an hour.'

'Shall I go and see?'

'Sure.'

Footsteps hardly sounded, although the mews had a cobbled surface. Only Ken stood near the corner, wide open to attack. Dawlish didn't move. Kate would soon be coming out to meet him.

The only light in the alley was a glow from her room.

The man returned from the *Blue Moon*, with nothing to report. They went and looked at the car again, and their voices travelled more clearly.

'He couldn't have gone to the flat.'

'Mobey would have seen.'

'I wish I knew what he was up to,' said Ken. 'I never trusted the swine. If I'd had my way—'

'*Look!*' exclaimed the other man.

The glow from Kate's window went out; now it was impossible to see more than a few yards along the alley. Ken said: 'Keep a sharp look-out,' and went along the alley towards Mobey. The padding sound of his footsteps quickly faded. The other man, five yards away from Dawlish, stood peering right and left.

The only sound now was the strains of music from the *Blue Moon*.

Dawlish slipped out and opened the front door. The catch clicked a trifle as he did so. Slowly he opened it wide. Soon he was able to see the man's dark shape, at the corner. He was facing the other way.

Dawlish took three long, silent steps, then thrust out his right hand and clutched the man by the throat. A faint gurgle came, rubber heels squeaked on the pavement. The man thumped back against Dawlish's chest, too startled to struggle. Dawlish kept up the pressure, felt the man's chest heaving, felt the muscles of his neck working as he tried to breathe. The man kicked backwards; the kicks hurt Dawlish's tender legs. But soon his victim weakened and grew limp. Dawlish maintained the pressure long enough to be sure that the other wasn't foxing.

When he released him, the man sank down, and would have fallen without Dawlish's aid.

Dawlish used the cord to bind his wrists and ankles, then lifted him, using his left hand gingerly, to the car. He pushed him into the back, made sure he couldn't be seen from the window, then quietly closed the door.

He hurried to the corner.

There was a glimmer of light; a pale rectangle showed against the pavement, revealed the lamp-post and made a long shadow of a man or woman. It was too vague for Dawlish to be sure which. He quickened his pace, and thought he saw Ken move forward.

Kate appeared.

The door closed behind her.

Dawlish was near enough to see her look right and left along the dark street, as if she were puzzled by the dead lamp. Then the men sprang at her out of the gloom. They gave no warning, jumped from a standing start. She fell, heavily, and cried out, but the cry was stifled by a hand at her throat.

Dawlish rushed into action.

A smashing blow from his right sent one man down. The other whirled round and ran into a second pile-driver. Kate sprawled on the ground, gasping. The man who'd first been hit came leaping at Dawlish, with a hand upraised, but ran into Dawlish's foot, and squealed as he shot backwards.

Kate started to get up.

Ken, the second man, was gathering himself for a spring. Dawlish let him come, side-stepped, tripped him up and grabbed him by the coat collar. He hauled him to his feet, and took the gun from his own pocket; his left hand was healed well enough for him to use like that.

'Put 'em up,' said Dawlish, poking the gun into the small of Ken's back.

Kate was swaying on her feet, and the other man was picking himself up. Dawlish said: 'Put your hands up, chum. Come here.' The man made as if to obey, then turned and raced towards the end of the alley. Ken had his hands stretched high above his head.

'Stop him!' cried Kate.

'Not worth it,' said Dawlish. 'We haven't done badly.' He poked the gun harder into Ken's back. 'Open the door, Kate, we'll take him upstairs.'

She took a long time to open the door. In the hall, the light showed an unfamiliar Kate. Her hair was dishevelled, there was a tiny scratch on her forehead and her clothes were rumpled.

'Lead the way,' he said.

A narrow flight of stairs was opposite the front door. Kate went up slowly, holding tightly to the banisters. Her stockings were laddered, her skirt covered with dust. Dawlish pushed Ken ahead of him.

They reached the landing, and Kate fumbled with another key.

'Any room without a window?' asked Dawlish.

'The—the bathroom.'

She led the way to it, across a small hall from which three doors opened. She leaned against the wall. The bathroom was tiled in dove grey, and there was a sunken bath.

Dawlish took more cord out of his pocket, and said to Ken:

'Step in the bath. And turn round.'

Ken obeyed; and Kate watched as Dawlish tied his wrists, made him lie at full-length, and then bound his ankles. It took him a long time, because his left hand was beginning to throb.

At last Dawlish and Kate were outside the bathroom. She led

the way, more steadily, into one long, narrow room; a beautiful room in dove grey and maroon, furnished with exquisite *Louis Quinze* pieces. She went to a graceful cabinet, and opened a door. Bottles clinked in her hand. Dawlish took them from her, then glasses, and poured whisky.

She drank greedily.

'Poor Kate,' said Dawlish, with a hint of laughter in his voice. 'Now you know what it's like. Who planned this little game? You or Martson?'

CHAPTER XIX

THE STRONG ROOM

'I told you we'd have to be careful of Ken.'

'How did he come to know about the arrangement?'

'We—we told him to watch Calder's house.'

'I thought you weren't going to use him.'

'Two of our men couldn't face it; we had to have someone.'

'You'd have been wiser working on your own,' said Dawlish. 'All right, all right, I know what's behind it. Martson doesn't trust me, maybe he doesn't trust you. He had to make sure we went straight to him with the precious document. And he told Ken to take us to him. Ken has his own ideas.'

Kate said: 'Ken's finished, now.'

'We'll worry about him later. Are you going to change?'

She went off quickly and a door opened but didn't close. He heard her walking about, other doors opening. He stayed where he was.

Kate was back in ten minutes, spick and span, fresh, vital. She'd put on the black suit he'd seen her in first.

'We'd better hurry.' She turned to the door. 'Have you got the keys?'

'Luscious, I have mixed with rogues before. I'll pick up those keys when I need 'em, and not a minute sooner.'

She didn't argue, although he could tell that he'd shaken her. They went downstairs, Kate leading the way.

The darkness made the alley look empty. He paused for a few seconds, but heard nothing. He took her arm, and they hurried along the alley towards the *Blue Moon*. Ponderous foot-steps sounded as they drew near it, and against the light at the night-club door a policeman's silhouette appeared, massive and helmeted. Dawlish went to the car, and said: 'Don't look in the back.' He drove off, towards Milton Square, but stopped a few yards from it, leaned over the seat, shone his torch, and saw the man's eyes open.

'Who's that?' Kate sounded nervous.

'A pal of Ken's, who won't do any more harm to-night,' said Dawlish. 'I'm going to stop the car in Milton Street, just before it runs into the Square. You'll stay in it until I get back.'

She didn't protest, and Tim was waiting in the porch of number 12, patient as the night was long. He handed the keys over.

'What now?' asked Tim. 'Wait and watch?' He tried to infuse some of the old spirit into his voice.

'My dear chap! I've a job for you. We're going to do a spot of burglary. Calder's house.'

They left the porch and went briskly towards the car. No one was about, but a policeman on his rounds might turn into the square at any moment.

'What are we after?' asked Tim.

'Documents, I'm told. It might or might not be true. Luscious is coming with us. Your job is decoy. Get them to open the front door, and keep 'em busy. I'll do the rest. We can't make hard plans,' said Dawlish. 'But there are four watchmen, according to all reports. All huskies. I think two of them will come to the door together, and they shouldn't take long to handle. I fancy the other two will have orders to stay by the strong room, come what may. We'll take 'em when we've passed the first hurdle. Use the ammonia bags.'

The car loomed up.

'Come on Kate,' said Dawlish.

They walked briskly towards Calder's house. Its new coat of cream paint glowed through the gloom, for there was a street lamp almost opposite. They walked up the three steps leading to the front door, and Dawlish pressed the bell. Then all three drew scarves over the lower part of their faces.

Footsteps sounded inside. Chains and bolts were drawn, and a man appeared; the vague figure against the shaded hall light, with a gun in his hand.

Tim tossed the first ammonia bag into his face, and as he staggered back, a second man rushed forward—and got the other bag in his face. The fumes got into Dawlish's eyes, and Tim's, but didn't stop them. The two guards were blinded and hardly put up a fight. One man tried to get away, rushing to the foot of the stairs, but Dawlish brought him down. The crash resounded; he felt sure an alarm had been raised.

No one appeared to have heard it. The guards, trussed up and gagged, could only glare at them.

All three were downstairs, past two locked doors. The keys had enabled them to open without trouble. Dawlish didn't need to refer to the plan.

They'd come down a short flight of stairs from a door underneath a massive staircase; there was another door in front of them. Dawlish examined it closely, looking for wires—part of the house was wired with burglar alarms.

Dawlish stared at the lock, large and formidable, almost an impossible obstacle without the keys. 'Much too easy. I don't like it. No, there's something wrong. We were warned of four guards. This is the final door before the strong room. There's a passage beyond this, then the strong room door itself. There must be something other than keys to open it.' He stood staring at the lock, and Kate clenched her hands, as if she had to relieve her nervous tension somehow.

Dawlish turned suddenly.

'Give me a hairpin?'

She drew out a hairpin, one of the old-fashioned kind. He straightened it, scratched the enamel off the end, then took a piece of paper from his pocket. He held one end of the hairpin in the paper, and then touched the metal surround of the lock.

A tiny blue flash spat out.

'Simple, isn't it? Not only electric control, but a live lock-mount. If I'd used the key, I'd have had a hell of a shock and there would have been a din enough to wake the neighbour-hood. Pop upstairs, Tim, and make sure there wasn't an alarm.'

Tim disappeared.

'Then we can't—get in,' said Kate.

'We might think of switching off the current,' said Dawlish. 'The main switch is in the butler's pantry; your draughtsman mentioned that. Wise chap.'

All was quiet. They found the main switch, and thereafter worked by the light of torches. Dawlish tested the lock again, to make sure that the electric control wasn't governed by a secondary electric supply. There was no flash. Opening the heavy steel door took all their strength, but it made no sound. When the gap was just wide enough for Tim to squeeze through, he went, carrying the ammonia bags.

Dawlish heard a sharp exclamation, then the popping of the bursting bags. He squeezed through, gun in hand, but the other two guards were reeling back; they gave no more trouble than the first pair.

Dawlish turned the key in the lock of the strong room door, hesitated, then stood to one side and pulled at the door. Kate moved forward, to stand in front of it. 'Move away,' he said, so harshly that she obeyed hurriedly. 'Lend a hand, Tim,' said Dawlish. Both men gripped the handle of the door and pulled; it began to move slowly.

'Keep well to one side,' warned Dawlish.

The door was open an inch; two inches. It would have been easier to get on the other side and push, but Dawlish kept pulling with his one good hand. Tim strained against it, too, grunting with the effort. The door was open more than a foot now; it must weigh tons. It was on a floor pivot, not ordinary hinges.

It was half-way open.

'Don't look inside,' Dawlish said to Kate. The veins on his forehead stood out; his arm was aching. Tim gasped, and said: 'Take it easy a moment.' They stood there, wiping the sweat from their forehead. The guards, huddled in a corner, tried in vain to look round.

They started again, and the door moved more freely when they leant all their weight on it.

Suddenly: *Hisss-hissssss!*

A tongue of flame, whitish red, shot out like a jet from a high-powered hose. It seared the air, sent a hot breath about them, hit the far wall at the height of a man's head; and then gradually died away.

No one moved.

The whole place reeked with the smell of burning.

Kate stood with her hands in front of her face, as if she had been burnt or blinded. Tim had a curious, blank look. Dawlish was the first to move. He wiped his forehead with the back of his right hand, then went to Kate's side.

'It's all right,' he said. 'We're in, danger's all over.'

She put a hand out to Dawlish, and he took it roughly. She fell forward against him, yielding, seeking protection, and he knew that whatever had happened before, she was now deeply affected; this had seared her with fear.

'Get a hold on yourself!' He pushed her away roughly, and she closed her eyes, then braced herself. She took a step towards the door, but drew back fearfully.

'Will there be anything else?'

'No, that's the last trick.'

'How did you—*know*?'

'There are all kinds of cute little dodges to stop burglars, and Calder wouldn't be behind in any of them,' Dawlish told her. 'There isn't another door, though. Care to go in first?'

'I think—you've earned it,' she said, with a glimmer of her usual smile.

The strong room was small; he could stretch out his arms and touch the walls in all directions. In one corner were some stout cardboard cartons. The walls were, in fact, lined with a dozen safes. Dawlish had one key still to use; he tried it in the smallest lock, and it was the right one. Inside a narrow drawer were the keys for the bigger safes.

'Any idea what this document looks like?'

'It's sealed with blue sealing-wax—a large legal envelope, that's all I know.'

'Any idea what else is here?'

'His valuables, I suppose. Jewels.'

'Want them while you're about it?'

She showed more spirit. 'No, just the envelope, that's all. Don't touch anything else.'

'All right,' said Dawlish.

Dawlish went to the nearest safe, tried several keys, and then found the one which turned the lock. Kate caught her breath as he pulled at the handle. He stood to one side, as a precaution, but nothing happened this time, and the door was easy to open. Inside were several jewel-cases, but no papers, nothing that Kate wanted. He didn't waste time, but tried other safes. Three, although locked, were empty.

'Time flies,' murmured Tim.

Dawlish opened another door. Tim went out to retrace his steps and make sure that all was quiet. There was no sound inside the strong room. Kate, with more colour in her cheeks, watched Dawlish with tense interest. Her eyes held a hungry look every time he opened a door; disappointment clouded them whenever he drew a blank. There seemed to be an unending succession of safes, some full, most containing two or three things. Then he opened one which was filled with papers.

Kate whispered: 'We're getting close.'

'No sealed envelope,' said Dawlish, and took one of the documents out. It was a lease for some land in Manchester. There were other leases, title deeds, copies of agreements; but nothing which was sealed up.

Only four safes remained.

Dawlish opened the next one—but he didn't see documents, jewel-cases, money, bullion—anything at all that he expected to see. He stared stupidly. Kate came to join him, brushed against his shoulder, and drew in her breath.

The safe was crowded with toys.

CHAPTER XX

THE SEALED ENVELOPE

There were hundreds of them, unwrapped, colourful, and gay. Tiny dolls, lead soldiers, model cars, lorries, jeeps, farmyard animals, trains, bridges, road signs—a conglomeration which would have made any child's eyes glisten. They were placed in orderly array on the shelves, not too crowded, rather as if on display in a shop window.

Tim came in.

'All clear,' he said. 'What—good Lord!'

'Children's delight,' said Dawlish. 'I didn't know that Calder acted as Santa Claus.' He picked up a small scarlet engine. It weighed heavily, and appeared to be of lead. The wheels went round when he tried them on the palm of his hand; the pistons between the wheels moved, even the tiny gadgets inside the fireman's cabin turned. 'Did you expect to find these, Kate?'

'I didn't dream—' she began, then cut the words short. She wasn't only surprised; she was badly shaken.

'Tim,' said Dawlish, 'take a few of these—one each of different models—and pack 'em in one of those old cartons.'

'Right.' Tim, asking no questions, got busy. Dawlish turned to the next of the unopened safes, pondering over the effect of the discovery on Kate. She seemed more interested in the toys than in the next safe, where the sealed envelope might be, and kept darting surreptitious glances at Tim.

Dawlish pulled open the next door.

The sealed envelope was there.

He took it out.

Kate's breath was warm on his cheek.

'That's it.'

Dawlish turned it over; both sides were blank. It was too large to go in his pocket. He unbuttoned his coat, tucked it into the waistband of his trousers, and buttoned his coat up again. Tim was making a neat, quick job of the packing, and had a small carton three-quarters filled.

'Any luck?' he asked.

'Yes. How many more different models?'

'Five,' said Tim, taking out a farm-cart.

They were soon ready. Tim folded the carton and carried it under his left arm. They went out of the strong room, and Dawlish called softly to the two bound guards, who glared up malevolently.

'We'll send someone to look after you.'

Tim and Kate were already near the foot of the steps which led from the electrically controlled door. They found the other bound guards behind the front door. Dawlish told them the same thing, while Tim opened the front door. Kate stood to one side of it, suggesting that it would be a long time before she would stand squarely in front of an opening door.

They walked quickly to the parked car. Kate got into the back, treading on the prisoner, who grunted but didn't protest loudly. She sank down in a corner and raised her legs off the man on the floor. Dawlish took the wheel, Tim sat with his box of toys on his knees.

Dawlish drove through the quiet night until they reached Jermyn Street, slid to a standstill, and sat for a few moments doing nothing. Tim opened the door. 'Wait, Tim,' said Dawlish.

There were several street lamps, but no lighted windows. A stray taxi passed them, travelling fast. Kate didn't move.

'No one seems to be about,' said Tim.

'Can't be too sure,' mused Dawlish. 'Have a look inside, will you?'

'Surely.' Tim got out, left the box of toys, which rattled, and went into the house. Dawlish lit a cigarette, and stared into the driving mirror. He'd turned it to an angle so that he could see Kate in it. It wouldn't surprise him if she drew a gun—but she seemed to accept the situation philosophically.

Tim came out.

'All clear on the landing. I didn't go inside the flat.'

'We'll do that together,' said Dawlish. 'Come on, Kate.' He held her door open.

They went quickly into the house and up the staircase, and paused outside Tim's flat. Tim put the box of toys on the floor, and opened the door. He sidled inside, and didn't immediately put the light on. When he did, the hall seemed very bright.

'Inside, Kate,' said Dawlish. 'Wait in the hall.'

He and Tim went cautiously into each room and looked round, but found no one. Dawlish kept an ear cocked for any move from Kate, but she made none. When they returned to the hall, she seemed much less tense. In the sitting-room, Dawlish poured beer for himself and Tim, a Gin and It for Kate. She sat down in an easy-chair.

'Are you always as careful as this?' she asked.

'When I'm dealing with your friends, yes. Well, we're safe and sound, we've the envelope and the toys. What shall we look at first?'

'Tim isn't in this,' Kate said slowly.

'Consider Tim and me as one,' Dawlish said, sinking into a vast arm-chair. He saw more clearly how Tim could help him to convince Kate he was really working with her.

He slid the envelope from his waistband and rested it on his knees. It looked so significant with the heavy blue sealing-wax, but there was nothing to suggest that it was worth the life of a man—of Mick Ryan. Yet inside this envelope was all that Martson, Steen, and Kate had wanted—it was one of the causes of all the trouble.

'Do we tear it open, cut it, or try to pretend that it hasn't been touched?' mused Dawlish. Kate made no suggestion. 'Cut, I think.' Dawlish took out a penknife and opened the blade.

'Damn it, I forgot,' he said, and stretched out for the telephone. He dialled 999, and Kate jumped to her feet. 'Police?' he asked when a man answered. 'I should go to Milton Square if I were you—Lord Calder's house.'

Dawlish slit the envelope open, inserted his fingers and drew out some thick sheets of paper; they looked like legal documents. Then he saw a die-stamp on the top one. It was a plain stamp; the wording was readable because it was ridged, but there was no colouring. He held it so that he could read it more closely. It was circular. There was a crest in the middle, and round the outside, the words:

From The Office of The Cabinet.

Dawlish looked at Kate. 'Government business. Did you know?'

She didn't answer.

Dawlish unfolded the document. It was folded like a legal agreement, and there was neat, almost copper-plate writing on one of the folds. He read:

Report of the Royal Commission on Drugs.

'What is it?' asked Kate.

'As if you didn't know. Poor liar. Sweet Kate. The plot unfolds.' He didn't open the document any farther, but thoughts chased one another swiftly across his mind. Odd, conflicting thoughts—conclusions, some of them. That this was drug-trafficking; the old business that was never new, but was frequently closed up and as frequently found a new opening. That Kate and Martson's organisation distributed drugs; that they were distributed with the toys, which would be a clever ruse—few better.

He wished he could lay his hands on the *Commission Salesman's* records book. Until he could, he must play along with Kate.

She said: 'Does it name Steen or Martson?'

'I haven't looked,' said Dawlish. 'Close-written document, and it would take too long to read now. I think I begin to see why it was so urgently needed. I don't yet see why it's worth as much as Calder's whole estate, but no doubt that will work out in time. Tim, we're on to a drug racket.'

'Never did like drugs,' said Tim, but he sounded disappointed. 'Hardly sensational. Ever since I can remember, they've been having White Papers on drugs and what not.'

'You shouldn't have let him know,' Kate said to Dawlish in a taut voice.

Tim laughed.

'We share everything.'

Dawlish knew that Tim wished he hadn't said that. It struck

a chord, brought the other, unpleasant things rushing to the surface. To hide his confusion, Tim picked up his tankard.

'You shouldn't have let him know,' repeated Kate. 'It's not safe.'

Tim lifted his tankard. 'This is made of silver, and it's heavy. It would make a nasty wound in your head, luscious.'

'He's dangerous,' said Kate. She stood up and went to the door, as if afraid that one of them would try to escape. 'He's either got to come in with us, or—'

'Curtains,' murmured Tim.

She continued to ignore him, and stared at Dawlish, half-accusing, half-challenging.

'Can't you see that I'm right.'

Dawlish's face took on a strange look; strange to Kate, if not to Tim. It became wooden; all the vitality which bubbled inside him, usually showing in his eyes and in his manner, dried up. He stared fixedly at Tim, who sat on the arm of a chair, and was curiously blank-faced too. But Tim's eyes weren't blank. The restlessness he felt, because of Dawlish and Helen, was right back. They had restored the old relationship, only for Kate to drive it away again.

'Pat, I don't quite see what you're driving at,' said Tim. 'Tell the woman she's had it, and telephone Trivett. He'd love to get his hands on that document. Confess how you got it, and all will be forgiven. He can take Kate to a lonely cell, and question her, and pick up the other people concerned. There's no need for you to go any farther with the racket.'

There wasn't, as far as Tim could see. He didn't know enough about the *Commission Salesmen*. He didn't know enough about the organisation—he didn't know how far Trivett had asked Dawlish to go.

'Shall I call Trivett?' asked Tim. His voice was harsh; he wasn't quite sure how this was going to work out.

'No!' exclaimed Kate. 'No. Pat—'

'I shouldn't, old man,' said Dawlish.

Tim went towards the telephone.

'Sorry, Pat,' he said in a dead voice. 'We've come to an end, I suppose. I'm going to tell Trivett what we found in Calder's strong room. I don't want to be difficult. No need for him to know we differed about it; he can believe you told me to call. Unless you'd rather speak to him yourself.'

He touched the instrument, looking all the time at Dawlish.

'Sorry, old chap,' said Dawlish, in a voice as stiff and wooden as his face. 'Yes, we've come to an end. Or we've started different roads, whichever you like. I've done a lot for the good of the community, as they say, and what have I got out of it?' He laughed, harshly. 'Kicks in the pants. Every time I've done something off my own bat, I've been reprimanded by the authorities. Every time I've got ahead of the police, they've been so jealous they've tried to prevent me from working again. I've turned sour on 'em, Tim. Sour on everything, if it comes to that. You. Fel. Life. I'm in it now to get what I can out of it. I'm sorry it's happened like this. It's a pity you told me about being in love with Felicity. If you hadn't lost your head, Felicity would know nothing about Helen—or Kate.'

Tim lifted the receiver.

'You've gone sour? Or turned *foul*? Corrupt inside and out.'

He looked at Kate as if he would gladly murder her, and then put his other hand towards the telephone.

'I am going to telephone Trivett,' Tim said, very deliberately.

Dawlish took out his gun.

CHAPTER XXI

BETWEEN FRIENDS

'Don't be a fool,' said Tim, and started to dial.

'Put that down,' said Dawlish.

'There's just one way to stop me,' said Tim.

Dawlish leapt from his chair. Tim snatched the instrument off the table and flung it at him but he brushed it aside. Tim swung a wild left at Dawlish's face, and only grazed his cheek. Dawlish drove his fist into Tim's stomach, jerking his head forward; he clipped him beneath the chin, and sent him staggering back, eyes rolling. Kate slipped past Dawlish, picked up the telephone, replaced the receiver, and put the instrument back on its table.

Tim hit the floor with a heavy thud.

'Sorry, Tim,' said Dawlish.

He turned the gun, struck Tim on the temple with the butt; Tim folded up, with hardly a groan. Dawlish stood looking down on him, his face very pale, and a queer glint in his eyes. He didn't see Kate, but felt her soft hand on his. She smoothed his grazed knuckles gently, caressingly.

'You shouldn't have let him see what was in it.'

'Don't be dull. Tim suspected what I was up to. It was—us or Tim. I'd better get a fortune out of this.'

'He'll have to die.'

Dawlish said: 'Yes.' He looked away from Tim, turned to the document, and held it up. 'How did Calder get hold of a confidential report of a Royal Commission, and how did you and Martson come to know he had it?'

'Martson will tell you.'

He seized her wrist tightly, pulled her to him so that their faces were very close together, and said in a hard, grating voice: 'You'll tell me. I'm in this too deep to take chances. I'm going to test the depth with every move I make.'

'All right, Pat. Don't hold so tightly.' He relaxed his grip, but didn't let her go. 'Calder was on the Royal Commission as well as in the—business. It's a fight between him and Martson for control of it—complete control. He wouldn't tell Martson what the Commission found out, whether they know who's behind it, whether they know how far it extends. It's very big. World-wide.'

'Exported with the toys?'

'Yes.'

'In Calder's strong room, you said you didn't dream something—and then broke off. What didn't you dream. What shook you so much when you saw those toys?'

'I didn't know Calder knew how we distributed the stuff.'

Tim stirred, but didn't open his eyes. He would fox, hoping that he would get a chance to turn the tables. Kate looked down at him, and said:

'Let me handle Tim,' she said. 'I can quite easily.'

'I'll see it through,' said Dawlish harshly.

It was a knife-edge of dilemma. How to handle Tim, leave him alive and safe, and at the same time, convince Kate that he was dead. Kate mustn't suspect what he was really doing until he knew all about the *Commission Salesmen* and the organisation; he hadn't yet taken it all in. Once Tim were free he'd tell Trivett; which didn't matter; and he'd tell Felicity, which might matter a great deal.

'All right,' said Kate. Somewhere, a clock struck. *One—two—three—four*. 'It's late. If we're going to take him away before it gets light, we'll have to hurry.'

She wouldn't leave him until he'd dealt with Tim. Then he thought of the toys; and a way out.

It wasn't difficult to carry Tim downstairs, over his shoulders, or to dump him into the back of the car. The other man was still there; his eyes glistened in the faint light. Dawlish took the wheel. Kate, saying nothing about the box of toys, slid in beside him. He let in the clutch. The longer he left 'remembering' the more convincing it would be; and much better, if she remembered for him.

He eased off the brakes.

Kate started and grabbed his hands. 'Stop!'

He stopped. 'What's up?'

'Those toys! They mustn't be found.'

'I'll put 'em away when I get back,' said Dawlish.

'No, don't chance it. I'll go and get them. I—' She had the door of the car opened.

'Are there drugs in those toys?' asked Dawlish, suddenly.

'Calder wouldn't have put duds in his safe.'

'That's about right,' agreed Dawlish. 'What drugs are they?'

'They vary according to the type of toy.'

'Oh. Any—quick-acting ones? Arsenic? Strychnine?'

'Some, yes. Almost everything, but it's mostly cocaine and heroin.'

'Do you know which toy contains which?'

'Yes.'

Dawlish said sharply: 'Pick out arsenic. It acts quickly. Bring a bottle of whisky and a glass. Hurry!'

He waited until she had gone into the house, then got out himself. He glanced at Tim, whose head lolled against the window; he was unconscious, not foxing. Dawlish hurried along the street, half-running, half-walking. He heard footsteps at the end of the road. In the Haymarket there were nearly always policemen; there would surely be one now. He reached the corner, and a constable almost bumped into him as the man turned from a doorway he had been examining.

'Constable! My name is Dawlish. Patrick Dawlish.'

'I know you, sir.'

'Telephone the Yard, at once. Ask them to telephone Superintendent Trivett on a matter of great urgency. They'll find a man on a building site in Burn Street. They're to send there a doctor with a stomach pump—he's been poisoned. And listen: if the man isn't there when they arrive, they're to hide until he turns up, and let whoever puts him there, get away. But the sick man must be treated at once. If you fall down on this, there'll be a man's life on your conscience.' Dawlish didn't wait to say any more, but hurried back to the car. He didn't want to run; if he sounded breathless it would warn Kate he had been up to something. He reached the car as the front door of the house opened. Kate came out, carrying the box in front of her.

He waited until she came up, took the box, and carried it round to his side. Then he put it on Tim's knees. Kate closed the door.

He drove off. 'Did you get an arsenic container?'

'Yes.'

'We'll take him to a building site near here. Give him a drink of whisky, and—'

'He'll be found.'

'He's got to be found sooner or later. The quicker we get him off our hands, the better. Any smarter idea?'

'All right.'

They pulled up near the site in Burn Street. A corner house had been knocked down. Dawlish dragged Tim out of the car. Kate went ahead, found the gate and hurried on to the site. When Dawlish arrived she was standing near the light of a street lamp, pouring whisky into the glass. He laid Tim down, and straightened his legs, and knelt beside him and supported his head and shoulders. Tim grunted and stirred.

'Wake up, old chap,' urged Dawlish.

Kate was tapping one of the toys against the glass; Dawlish didn't see any powder; she was too far away. She kept tapping, and he called: '*Quieter!*' Tim opened his eyes, and Dawlish said: 'All right, Tim, I'm sorry I had to do that. I'm going to give you a drink.'

He took the glass and put it to Tim's lips.

Tim sipped.

Kate bent over them, gripped Tim's nose and threw his head back; his mouth gaped open. 'Toss it down,' she said. Dawlish emptied the glass, a little whisky came out of Tim's mouth; he gulped as it ran down his throat.

Tim stopped spluttering. Dawlish rested his head gently on the ground. Kate said: 'He must have been heard. Hurry.'

They reached the street safely. No one appeared to be about. But as he started off Dawlish thought he saw a man standing in a doorway; then a small private car came slowly along Burn Street. He didn't look at the driver or at Kate as he turned towards Piccadilly.

What had he done? Could anything justify it, if Tim died?

She rested a hand on his arm; cool, soothing, restful; or that was what she intended.

She hadn't had a moment's compunction. Even now he could picture her gripping Tim's nose and hear her telling him to toss the poison down. Supposing something went wrong? Supposing that policeman had failed him?

'Where are we going?' he asked gruffly.

'*My* flat,' said Kate, firmly.

In a dark alley he hid the man from the back of the car, then drove to the mews. There was no light over the entrance of *The Blue Moon*, no music broke the quiet. He led the way along the dark street. The lamps were still out; and Martson may have sent someone else to wait for them.

There was no attack.

Kate unlocked the front door and stood aside for him to enter. She was herself again; it was hard to believe that she had ever been shaken out of her poise.

Upstairs, she switched on a light. When the door closed behind them, she leaned against him, and smiled into his eyes.

'You need a drink.' She poured out whisky and sodas, and it wasn't until he'd drunk half of his that he thought of the possibility of being drugged.

He said nothing; she appeared quite unconcerned—but gradually weariness stole over him.

'Kate, have you—'

'Just a little veronal,' she said. 'You need rest.'

He could have killed her. For she could do what she liked with that document.

It was broad daylight when he woke up, and found himself alone, in Kate's bed.

'So, you see, you're alive,' said Kate. She stood in the doorway; a dream of beauty. She wore a quilted dressing-gown of gay colours which suited her. Her hair rippled down to her shoulders, and made her look years younger. She had on little make-up. When she came towards him he saw that she didn't wear much else. But it was almost impossible to believe that this radiantly beautiful woman had held Tim's nose last night and thrown back his head.

Tim!

He struggled up. 'Any news? What time is it?'

'Half-past twelve. No, there's no news.' She took the long envelope from inside the dressing-gown. 'I haven't run off with this, you see.'

'Did you mean to?'

'You thought I would. Pat, I'm all for you.'

'Thanks,' he said. He licked his lips and ran his fingers over his stubble. He knew he looked a sight. This was a dainty room, beautifully furnished in pastel colours, light and fresh; and he was unshaven, probably dark-eyed, just a brute of a man. 'I want a shave.'

'The kettle's on for some tea.'

'So you're domesticated,' he said.

'You're only just beginning to know me,' Kate assured him lightly. 'I won't be long.'

When she came back she brought the morning papers. There was nothing about the robbery or Tim—he didn't expect to find anything. Kate left him, saying he would find a razor and everything he needed in the bathroom. That reminded him of the prisoner.

'I've sent Ken away,' she explained. 'You needn't worry about him any more.'

He didn't ask what poison she had used.

He bathed and shaved, with thought of Tim obsessing him. Just after one-thirty, she came into the bedroom again, fully dressed. She had an evening paper in her hand.

He didn't read the headline, the second one about Lord Calder that week, but looked at the stop press to which she pointed.

'Body of a man, believed poisoned, found in a building site in Burn Street early this morning. The police suspect foul play.'

CHAPTER XXII

THE TOYS

The police-constable must have garbled the message. Kate might have put something quicker-acting than arsenic into the whisky, something which couldn't be pumped out of the stomach in time. He was to blame for the deadly notion; it was one thing to take a chance with his own life, but Tim—

'I'll have to go to Tim's flat,' he said. 'We were friends, we've always worked together. No sense in disappearing. They'll put a call out for me because they'll think I've been kidnapped. They'll probably also look for my body.' He pushed his fingers through his hair. 'Does Martson know we pulled it off?'

'He reads the newspapers.'

She'd telephoned Martson, of course.

Dawlish glanced at the headline, and read the story of the four outwitted bodyguards at Lord Calder's house. The account made it seem as if they had been battered almost to death, made them out to be heroes who had fought to the bitter end. He tossed the paper aside.

'There are some things we have got to get straight. I'm in fifty-fifty, with Martson. You're playing with both of us at the moment. Whose side are you really on?'

'I wish you'd trust me,' said Kate, 'It's really very simple. Martson has everything under his thumb, and Steen used to have. They've often used me as a decoy, but I've never been taken fully into their confidence. Only that it's drug traffic, and there's a world-wide organisation. I know they distribute through a big toy firm, with a large export business. I don't know which one. I know there are representatives who travel the country and peddle the stuff at the same time as they sell toys. I don't know who they are. The police have been looking for the organisation. You can't conceal the fact that drugs are being peddled for long. The police know it's extensive. They were so worried that the Home Office went into it, and asked for a Royal Commission on the distribution as well as the control and effects of certain drugs. Calder has worked with Martson for a long time. He got scared. About six months ago he broke with Martson. We tried to bring him to heel, but he shut himself up in his house, and wouldn't give us a chance. He wanted to be left alone, to forget it. Martson threatened blackmail, but Calder would have put him inside. It was checkmate. Then Calder managed to steal the first report of the Commission, together with all copies and drafts. He said it hadn't even been read by the Cabinet—certainly not considered. I don't know how he did it. He told Martson that the report was in his strong room and would stay there for as long as he needed it. He even described the envelope. He said there was enough in it to expose Martson, Steen, and the whole organisation. You see how important it was. We had to get it, and find out whether it was true.'

'Was it?'

She laughed. 'No! Calder was pulling a fast one. The report says there must be clever distribution and it goes on prosily to explain how dangerous it is and how widespread, but it doesn't put a finger on anyone. If it hadn't been for finding those toys, I'd have said that Calder was just bluffing. He's not. He knows how we distribute and might know the firm. If the police were to get hold of those toys, they'd find the wholesalers and soon they'd trace the salesmen, then the firm. That wouldn't do, would it?'

'So we're not out of the jam yet.'

'Calder won't use those toys, provided we let him alone.'

'I wish I were so sure.'

Kate came closer. 'Pat, I know Calder. If he thinks he's safe, he won't do any harm. He's terrified of Martson and was frightened of Steen. Steen's gone. If Martson goes—'

'That's how it always happens. One murder leads to another. Aren't you ever satisfied.'

'We can't be satisfied or safe while Martson's alive, but he mustn't die until we know all about the distribution. That's obvious, isn't it? So I'm going to take the document to Martson. Tell him how wonderful you've been. Make sure that he believes in you. Then it'll be up to you to find out how he sells the stuff, how big the distributing organisation really is. You can do that with one eye shut. Martson already has a great respect for you.'

'Yes. And fixes Ken to spy on me.'

'Naturally. He didn't know that Ken would turn like he did.'

'Where's Ken now?'

She shrugged her shoulders. 'Do you have to know all about it? The only man who can do us any harm is Mobey, who escaped. Ken and the man who was in the back of your car— don't worry about them.'

Dawlish said: 'All right. When are you going to see Martson?'

'Now.'

'I'll wait here until you come back.'

When she had gone, he sat for a few minutes in an easy-chair, his face drawn and haggard.

He looked at the telephone. A talk with Trivett might help.

But he might be under close observation, the telephone might be tapped. It was even possible that it was tapped without Kate knowing it. What was Kate really planning?

He went to the box of toys, and took several out.

He picked up a steam-engine, and tapped it both ends, but no powder came out. He fiddled with the gadgets—and suddenly a trace of powder appeared on his hand.

The powder came through the funnel when one of the control wheels was moved.

He tapped out a little more. It was a white powder; was it cocaine or heroin, one of the narcotics? Or strychnine or arsenic? He didn't taste it, but studied it for some time. Then he took out a car, and several other toys, wrapped them in a handkerchief, and thrust them into his pocket. They made a little bulge. Then he looked through the flat. There was nothing of interest; nothing that helped him in his quest.

And once he'd had the sales book in his hand!

He'd even let Kate go, without first reading the report of the Royal Commission, because he was so anxious to make her believe that she could rely on him, that they were really working together. She was almost certainly double-crossing him.

It wouldn't be any use having those toys in a dead man's pocket.

He hunted for a small box; found one; put the toys in it, and wrapped it up in brown paper. Then he addressed it to Trivett, at the Yard. He went to the window; he hadn't looked out of it that morning. The alley looked bleak in daylight. The broken lamp opposite hadn't been mended, and the splinters of glass still lay on the pavement. He leaned out of the window, but no one was in the alley. He might be under observation from across the road, but no one was lounging in Wickin Lane itself.

Now and again a car passed along the lane. Two or three

women, middle-aged, also went by. He would have given a lot to see the familiar blue helmet of a policeman. Then a small open two-seater appeared. A girl sat at the wheel, a fair-haired creature with a gay scarf fluttering behind her. She was driving slowly, looking for a number of a house.

He judged the moment, tossed the packet out, and held his breath. It fell into the back of the car. He couldn't tell whether the girl had noticed the thud. He stood by the window, watching the car. It stopped, she went to a near-by house, with a letter in her hand, delivered the letter and drove off again.

The packet might lie unnoticed for days.

He lit a cigarette—and the telephone bell rang.

He shrugged his shoulders, and went across and lifted the receiver.

Kate said: 'Pat, I've seen Martson. He's delighted, but he doesn't want to come to see you there. He'll see you later in the evening, after dark. I'm staying with him all day, but I'll meet you at eight o'clock.'

'Where?'

'Outside the *Crown*, the other end of Wickin Lane. The saloon bar. Pat, he thinks you ought to go to Tim's flat, and act as if nothing had happened.'

He was followed by a middle-aged, drab-looking woman, who didn't leave him until he was outside the Jermyn Street flat.

He walked heavily up the stairs. Everything seemed normal; there were no signs of the police, nothing to indicate that anyone knew who the dead man in Burn Street had been. *Had* been. Here was the flat which Tim and he had shared when they had first started to work together, with M.I.5. It had been his and Felicity's first home; Tim had stayed at his club, so that the newly-weds should have a place in which to share their lives. Everything was familiar; the front door had a friendly look.

Then he remembered that he'd given Kate the keys when she had come up for the toys. He tapped his pockets, in vexation, and stared at the door, willing it to open.

He hardly knew why he pressed the bell.

Someone stirred inside the flat; a man's footsteps approached the door. Dawlish drew back, and his heart began to thump wildly.

'Hallo, Pat,' said Trivett.

Dawlish went in, and Trivett closed the door.

Trivett said: 'What's the matter, Pat?'

He turned round. 'Do you have to ask? I thought I could rely on the police. God, what a fool I was! Didn't they give you the message? Did you ignore it? What the devil did happen? Is the show worth *this*?'

Trivett said: 'Steady, old chap. Tim's all right, you know.'

CHAPTER XXIII

MARTSON APPROVES

Dawlish raised his hands; dropped them again.

'He's feeling a bit dicky, of course; you would be if you'd had the stomach pump in you.' Trivett laughed a little. 'He doesn't think a lot of you, Pat, but that can be put right later. He made a statement and told me all about it—that's why I had the body reported.'

Dawlish dropped into a chair.

'Bad strain, isn't it?' asked Trivett. 'I'm sorry, Pat, but I think it's the only way. I'd trust Tim and Felicity with anything, but— well, safe's safe. You got the document from the strong room, I suppose? Was it the Royal Commission's report?'

'It was, William.'

How different he felt! All was right with the world—even with Trivett, who had given him such a bad time. Tim was alive, and—

'Where is it now?'

'Martson has it. Kate took it to him this morning.'

'So you're well in with them?'

'I wouldn't say that yet. Do you know Kate?'

'A little. She's Kate Lehmann. Friend and probably mistress of Calder and several others who've suffered at Martson's hands. We know very little about Martson. We knew more about Steen. His body was taken out of the river two days ago. He'd been inside three times—once for drug distribution, twice for bucket-shop frauds. He was an extremely dangerous man. He's run several gangs, all of them killers, but we'd never been able to get him.'

'Where does Martson come in?'

'He was at one time secretary of *Calder's Combined Trust*. Irreproachable reputation, at the time. His reputation in the City was first class. There was keen competition for his services before he went to Calder. He's believed to be one of our best financial brains. Just where he and Calder started to take the wrong turning, I don't know,' Trivett said. 'We've been suspicious of Calder for some time. We can't find anything wrong with the financial standing of the *Trust* or any of his companies, and yet—well, you know how rumours spread. We've watched him. We had a pretty shrewd idea that he'd lifted that report, but—'

'When a peer of the realm goes bad, treat him cautiously.'

'It wasn't only that. We weren't sure. We had Home Office instructions, anyhow.' Trivett opened the secret door an inch. 'We didn't know—we still don't know—just how far this business has gone. Whether drugs is the beginning and the end, or whether there's something else. Any hint of anything else?'

Trivett did know more, but wouldn't tell.

'No,' said Dawlish, then frowned. 'I don't know, though. Kate once said that what we found in Calder's safe would be worth more than Calder possessed, and I wouldn't have said that even a world-wide drug-trafficking racket would hit those figures. What is he worth?'

'At a rough estimate, ten million pounds.'

'Well, well,' breathed Dawlish. 'I wouldn't like to pay ten million pounds for the drug organisation, would you?'

'No.'

'Then probably there is something else. Which,' said Dawlish, leaning back against the wall, 'is where we really started. She might be pulling a fast one over me. I've gone as far as I can to convince her that I've turned into a rogue. She seems to believe it. But whether she's really fooling me, I don't know. When she was attacked last night, it looked as if Ken—Steen's section—had turned against her, because she was working with me, and because Steen's death was my doing. That might be true. On the other hand, it might have been to convince me that she was in danger. Bill, the truth is that I don't yet know whether I'm really well in with Kate, or whether she's planning to use me and then double-cross me. She talks about getting the details of the organisation from Martson, and then killing him. She and I will then be lords of all we survey. But—' He shook his head.

Trivett smiled grimly. 'I can imagine what you feel like, Pat. And some things aren't so good. Felicity and Tim, I mean, but—that *will* be put right. I'm rather surprised that Felicity has jumped to the worst conclusions so quickly.'

Dawlish said: 'I suppose I am, too. She didn't really believe me when I told her that I'd never heard of Ryan until I discovered his body.'

'Would even that be enough to upset her so much?'

'It could be. What are you getting at?'

'I don't know. I'm all mixed up, Pat, but some things are crystal clear. One, that you've got to go on with this until you've learned everything about the organisation, and dug deep enough to find out its real purpose—if there's one we don't know. Have you met Calder? It might be a good idea, you know. See what chance crops up. When are you seeing Kate again?'

'To-night at eight. Pub at the corner of Wickin Lane.'

'All right. Keep things going as they've started, and stay away from Felicity. Tim won't come back here, by the way. I've arranged for the "body" to be nameless, so there won't be anything in the Press about Tim himself. Kate will assume it's because we know he's a friend of yours. We'll keep him at the hospital for a few days—I think he'll see the sense of that.'

'I hope so,' said Dawlish. 'What else are you doing?'

'Helping the build-up,' said Trivett. 'We had a squad of men here early this morning—and others will be here soon. I slipped in with the crowd, sent the others off, and waited for you. Two or three more will soon come and I'll slip out with them. I don't think anyone will know I was lying in wait. Is there anything else you can tell me?'

'One thing,' said Dawlish. He told Trivett about the toys which he had thrown into the back of the two-seater; a wasted effort, because he could as easily have brought them here and handed them to Trivett.

'They'll turn up,' said Trivett. 'Where will you go from the *Crown*?'

'I've no idea. I'll let you know as soon as I can.'

'All right,' said Trivett. 'Pat, I know it's tough, but remember—you're not working alone.'

It was a cosy little pub. The saloon bar was an oak-panelled, oak-beamed room, with many small tables dotted about, a comfortable haze of tobacco smoke and a smell of beer.

Dawlish ordered a mild-and-bitter, and stood at the bar, listening with half an ear to the hum of conversation, the friendly greetings of the motherly old barmaid behind the bar to all the new-comers, the tit-bits of gossip and scandal that were tossed to and fro. He began to feel restive.

A little man came in, looked round, and came towards him. He shuffled up to the bar, ordered a mild-and-bitter, and while he was waiting for it, looked furtively at Dawlish and whispered out of the corner of his mouth:

'They're at Killiger Street.'

The shop at the corner was in darkness, but a street lamp showed that the tinned goods were piled up in the window in colourful towers, exactly the same as Dawlish had seen them when he had taken shelter with Helen. He walked towards number 41, but before he reached it another little man came out of the shadow of a doorway and said huskily:

'They're at sixty-three.'

'They' had a surprising number of scouts.

It was Mulligan who opened the door to him at number 63.

More than anything else, that brought a warning of danger to Dawlish. Mulligan and Ken had much in common, Ken was supposed to be hostile now, but Martson still used Mulligan.

Mulligan grunted. 'Upstairs, first door on the left.'

The house was exactly the same as number 41 except that it seemed fresher and cleaner. There was a light on the landing and a light under the door of the room on the left. He didn't tap, but tried to open it; it was locked.

He thumped on the door.

Kate opened it, and greeted him as if she had been longing for this moment. 'Pat!' She gripped his hand and drew him into a well-lighted room. It was a combination office and sitting-room—and the desk at which Martson sat was very like the one in number 21 Elkin Street: small, with shiny walnut veneer and with some books and papers on the top. One of the books looked familiar, and although it was upside down to him, he read the words: '*Commission Salesmen.*' He began to feel better.

'I'm very glad to see you, Dawlish, very glad,' said Martson. He stood up, looked as if he were going to offer his hand, and thought better of it. He dropped back into his chair. He looked the part of a financier, with his bald head and pale face, his neat dark-grey suit. 'Kate's been telling me all about it, and you've worked wonders.'

'That's fine,' said Dawlish. 'Where do we go from here?'

'How you remind me of Steen,' cooed Martson. 'He was always like that, anxious to get on with the job.' His manner was that of a senior wrangler towards a very dull undergraduate to whom he wanted to be friendly. 'There's plenty to do, Dawlish, plenty. Kate's told you that I've had a little trouble with Lord Calder. There was a time when Kate used to take messages from me to Calder,' said Martson, with a sigh. 'It was all so easy then, he worked with us. Then he turned against her, so I had to send Steen. And now poor Steen is dead. I'd like you to go and see him, Dawlish. He doesn't know you, so he'll receive you. As a matter of fact, *I* want to speak to him myself.'

'Just a simple kidnapping, is that it?'

'How quick you are! *Do* you think you could bring him here?'

'Supposing I bring him, what then?'

'What happens will depend on whether we can make him see reason,' said Martson gently. 'I think we shall. The whole situation is now very straightforward. Either Calder must join us again, or—well, it will be unfortunate for him. He must let us have that safe-ful of toys, of course; he mustn't be allowed to keep those.'

'I still don't get it,' said Dawlish. 'What good will Calder be to us?'

Martson actually laughed; it was a hoarse, cracked sound.

'You'd be surprised! We can manage without him, but he

can make or mar our plans, Dawlish. After all, you have a big interest in their success now, haven't you? Fifty per cent! You must earn it. You know that very large profits are to be made out of the business, but—it needs someone to keep it going. I am not an active man, like Steen was—you replace Steen.'

Dawlish said: 'I'm an equal partner.'

'Yes, yes. Of course.'

'I don't intend to be double-crossed.'

'My dear Dawlish! You don't get the idea at all. We *need* you. After all,' murmured Martson, 'the situation is rather different now from what it was. When you first came to see me—well, I couldn't be sure of you. You were untried, and suspected of working with the police.' Was that a sneer, was he really telling Dawlish that he knew he still was? 'Now, things have altered! After all, you killed Steen. And you—ah—killed your friend Jeremy. You're prepared to do murder—you have done murder. It was kill or be killed. So of course I trust you to work well with me.'

He didn't add aloud: 'Or you'll find yourself charged with murder,' but that was exactly what he meant.

Kate, who had been standing near the desk, came forward and said sweetly:

'It's getting late. If you're going to see Calder to-night, you ought to go, Pat. She looked at Dawlish as if she were trying to tell him that this fitted in with their own particular plot.

'And supposing he won't come?'

'You see how much we trust you—we know you'll bring him,' said Martson, and looked at his watch. 'Kate's right, it's turned nine o'clock. Have you a car with you, Dawlish, or would you like to use Kate's?'

Kate's car was in a garage at the far end of Killiger Street. What more natural than that she should walk with him to the garage, holding his arm, making him vividly aware of her closeness.

'You've won Martson over, Pat, he'll eat out of your hand. I don't know why he wants Calder, but it's important. When you've got Calder, we'll be able to control everything. We'll just step into Martson's shoes. It won't be long, now.'

Kate squeezed his arm.

She opened the door of the lock-up garage, and he drove the car out. She closed and locked the door and then got in next to him. He drove the purring car along Killiger Street, and drew up outside number 63. It was very dark, although the night was bright and the stars pricked the sky. She didn't get out immediately.

'We'll have such a wonderful future, Pat.' She leaned against him, and her face was turned towards his. The night made dullness everywhere, and yet her eyes glistened. 'Won't we?'

His arm slid round her shoulders.

'Wonderful!'

He kissed her; her lips parted, to give the kiss full meaning, full delight, and then she broke away from him and slid out into the darkness.

CHAPTER XXIV

JEREMIAH

Dawlish parked his car two doors along, and walked to Calder's house.

He rang the bell.

He was quite sure that the guards wouldn't recognise his features, but they might recognise his figure. Did that matter much now? Trivett would take no action, even if he were consulted, and Calder had done all he could to keep the police out.

A footman opened the door; young, sleek, smiling.

'Good evening, sir.'

'Is Lord Calder in?'

'I'll inquire, sir.' The footman stood aside. Lights from a glass chandelier sparkled in the hall. A man sat in a chair near the door, reading a book. He looked as if he were waiting to see Calder, and this were a waiting-room; he was actually one of the guards, big and clumsy-looking. He glanced up at Dawlish, then down at his book.

The footman showed Dawlish into a magnificent drawing-room, a stately chamber with stately furniture and concealed lighting; and took Dawlish's card.

He was gone for five minutes. Then:

'His lordship can see you, Mr. Dawlish.'

'Thanks.'

'If you will please come this way.'

There was a hush about the house. The carpets had a thick pile, deadening all sound; it was like entering a sanctuary. On the walls were masterpieces; not just good paintings, masterpieces. Not a piece of furniture was ordinary, yet there was no ostentation.

The footman led the way up to the spacious first-floor landing, then to a door on the right. He tapped and opened the door.

'Mr. Dawlish, my lord.'

Dawlish went in to see Jeremiah—and that was a shock, because all his preconceived notions went by the board. He had expected a wizened old man, crabbed by his money, harassed by his multitudinous interests. Instead, the man who stood up behind a magnificent Regency desk was almost as tall as he. Nor was Calder old—at least, nothing in his erect figure or his greying hair suggested age; he might be somewhere between fifty and sixty, probably nearer fifty.

He smiled, charmingly.

'Good evening, Mr. Dawlish.'

'Good evening,' said Dawlish heavily.

He felt as if he were looking at a Greek god; a god brought back to life, rejuvenated, full of vitality; a personality. There was a hint of a smile at Calder's lips—perhaps, also, a touch of mockery.

'How can I help you?'

Dawlish said: 'I hope we can help each other.'

'Really? But sit down, Mr. Dawlish.' There was brandy on the desk, and a small electric fire burned, warming two glasses—almost as if a visitor had been expected. 'A little brandy?'

'Thanks, I will.'

'I've often heard of you, and often wanted to meet you,' said Lord Calder, and the smile now seemed to be in his voice. 'You have such an outstanding reputation, Mr. Dawlish. And no doubt you have come about the two robberies I've had here.' He picked up the glasses, bending his knees, not stooping down to get them. They glowed in his hands. 'I am told that you are not always patient with the police.'

'Seldom,' said Dawlish.

'Then we're on common ground.' The brandy gurgled into the glasses; Calder passed one across, picked up the other and inhaled the bouquet, but didn't drink. 'Am I right in saying that your interest has been tittivated by the two incidents here? And you've come to offer help?'

'Possibly.'

'So that's what you meant when you said that you hoped we could help one another, Mr. Dawlish; I hope you won't mind complete frankness. I read the newspapers, you know. I saw a few days ago that my secretary—poor Mick, I was so sorry for him of late, he'd been so changed—was found murdered near your house, and it occurred to me that Mick had been bringing his problem to you.'

'He had.'

'Thank you. I don't quite know what that problem was,' said Calder thoughtfully, and he sipped, paused, as if in reverence before the brandy. 'I know he was troubled; I think it was because he was under pressure to spy upon me. Young men are careless, you know, and are easy to blackmail. I suspect that he was so worried that he daren't go to the police. Knowing your reputation and your good nature, he came to see you—and was killed before he reached the house. Isn't that so?'

He was trying to find out whether Mick Ryan had told Dawlish anything about him.

'Yes.'

'And you have been probing into the mystery.'

'Yes,' said Dawlish.

'I wonder how far you have got,' murmured Calder. 'I'm afraid that the evidence shows that Mick was foolish enough to take my keys and let someone else have a duplicate set. Otherwise, last night's robbery would not have succeeded—those doors were opened with keys. However, no great harm was done, nothing of importance was taken.'

Yes, he was really trying to find out whether Dawlish knew what had been taken.

'The second lot of thieves had the same bad luck as the first. Your good luck.'

'Ah, yes.' Calder sipped again. 'How far have you got with your investigation, Mr. Dawlish? As far as'—his smile was charming, it made him look young and almost jaunty—'Kate Lehmann?'

It was easy to believe that Kate had been this man's mistress.

'A woman named Kate,' said Dawlish.

'And you know that we were once friendly, you know that she isn't exactly all that a woman ought to be, and that she has been in touch with criminals,' said Calder. 'So now you're wondering whether I can't give you more information, and enable you really to get your teeth into the problem. Is that it?'

He spoke precisely, marshalling facts almost as if he had rehearsed them; and his voice was mellow and pleasing.

'You've got the idea exactly,' said Dawlish.

'Good! I confess that when I heard that you'd called, I wondered whether we could work together,' said Calder. 'And yet—I think I'm capable of handling my own affairs, Mr. Dawlish. You mustn't believe all that you read or all that Kate tells you about me, you know. You never suspect the truth about her until it's—almost too late. But I was just in time, Mr. Dawlish.'

'Were you?' asked Dawlish gently.

The hint of a smile faded, and Calder cupped his hands tightly about his glass. His voice sharpened.

'Yes, I was.'

'I don't think so. I've turned up the proper mud,' said Dawlish, and smiled in turn. 'Thick, oozing, slimy mud, which is going to stick tight if anyone starts throwing it about. Kate learned more than you realised.'

'What—what do you imagine she learned?'

'I'll show you what she learned if you'll come with me,' said Dawlish.

'You can tell me what it is.'

'This is one of the things you have to see for yourself.'

What should he do if Calder refused to come? Frighten him? One could never tell with a man who was so artificial, but he thought Calder would be scared of a gun.

'Where is this—discovery?'

'Not far away.'

'I don't see why I should come with you.' Calder sounded almost petulant now.

'Don't be a fool,' said Dawlish roughly. 'I tell you that Kate learned a lot more than you realised, and hasn't kept it to herself. I can show you the evidence, all the accumulation of muck. And I think I can avoid a scandal. I've given you a break. Take it or leave it.' He stood up. 'Are you coming?'

It couldn't be as easy as this.

'I'll come and see what you mean, but I don't commit myself to anything else.'

There was something wrong; he couldn't think what it was.

* * *

Of course, Calder agreed to come because he was frightened. But was that the whole truth? Had he some other reason for giving way? The possibility twisted and turned in Dawlish's mind as he drove from Milton Square with Calder by his side. A saloon car which had been parked along the square followed. Calder had doubtless arranged to be followed everywhere. Perhaps that was one reason why he came; although frightened, he felt physically safe.

It wasn't difficult to shake the saloon car off.

Dawlish wasn't sure whether Calder realised that it was no longer following.

Killiger Street was darker and gloomier, because clouds were being driven across the sky and the stars were blotted out. Dawlish saw no lurking figures, although he had little doubt that as soon as the car turned into the street, Kate and Martson were told about it.

He drew up outside number 63.

Calder looked behind him, as if nervously seeking his bodyguard.

The door opened as they approached, and Mulligan sniffed again. Calder glanced at the man, but hardly seemed to notice him. The door upstairs was open and light came through. No one spoke. The sound of music, soft and gentle, came from the room.

Mulligan rammed home the bolt at the door, then fitted a chain into position.

Kate appeared at the head of the stairs. She smiled down at Dawlish: Calder was looking the other way, and didn't see her. Her smile said: 'Wonderful, we're nearly through.' Then she called:

'Jeremiah, darling.'

It was the familiar bewitching voice. It made Calder swing round and stare, as if he could not believe his ears.

'I'm so glad to see you,' said Kate.

Calder opened his mouth, but couldn't speak. He gripped Dawlish's arm, and tried to push past him, ignoring Mulligan, who stood with his back to the door.

'Come up, darling,' cooed Kate. 'We only want a little talk. Pat, make him come up.'

'*Pat!*' echoed Calder.

'Didn't he tell you we were such good friends?' asked Kate. 'He must have forgotten. We only want a little talk, darling. A round-table conference, so to speak—you and me, Martson and Dawlish. Between us, we ought to do very well indeed, oughtn't we?'

Calder swayed against Dawlish.

'*I'll* make 'im,' growled Mulligan.

'Better go up,' said Dawlish. 'I promised to show you plenty, didn't I?' He gripped Calder's arm just above the elbow, propelled him towards the stairs and then up them. Calder's legs were unsteady, and he went up one by one. He wasn't trembling; he had firm muscles, was a man in good physical condition.

Was this an act?

A darker shadow of doubt clouded Dawlish's mind. Did he really know why Calder had been brought here?

'Come along,' called Kate.

She waited by the open door, and when Calder reached it, linked her arm through his and walked into the room. Martson sat at the desk, grinning up like a pale-grey ogre. No one else was in the room. Dawlish followed and closed the door behind him.

'*Very* nice work, Dawlish,' said Martson. 'Don't you think he'll do better than Steen?'

'Better—' began Calder, and swung round. Kate clung on

to his arm, or he would have struck Dawlish. 'Is he—working for *you*?'

'Our new partner,' purred Martson.

'His reputation is such a help,' said Kate.

'Now you know all about that, come and sit down,' said Martson, pointing to a chair in front of a small fireplace with a gas fire. 'You sit down, Dawlish—you've earned a rest.'

'Pat can work miracles,' murmured Kate.

'I'm beginning to think so.' Martson folded his hands and rested them on the desk, half-turning in his seat so that he could see Calder. 'Now, here we are, all together. We will have to come to terms—reach a working agreement. After all, we managed to get along very well in the past; I don't see why we shouldn't again. We've lost a lot of time and a great deal of profit by quarrelling,' said Martson reasonably. 'It's much better that we pool all our resources. I confess I haven't been happy while we've been parted. It's true I have the drugs and the business sewn up, but while an enemy—and there's no worse enemy than a renegade friend, is there?—knew so much about it, I didn't feel safe. Don't you think it's time you worked with us again, Calder?'

'I've finished with you,' muttered Calder.

'I don't want you to take that attitude,' Martson purred. 'If you do, you won't leave here alive. I know you don't want to die just yet—why, you're in the prime of life! And such an important person. It wouldn't do, Calder. Now, let me assess the situation for you. We know you stole the *Royal Commission's report*, and if that were proved you'd be ruined. We know you have a store of the toys, and perhaps you think that cancels out anything we have against you.'

'They'll find you through those toys,' said Calder, but he didn't sound sure, and looked desperately afraid. *Looked*.

'Perhaps they could, but—we mustn't keep talking at

cross-purposes,' murmured Martson. 'No, indeed. You know what we really want, don't you?'

Calder kept silent.

'And we're going to have it,' insisted Martson.

Whatever this unknown 'something' was, Dawlish knew nothing about it. But Calder did. So did Kate, who was smiling secretively to herself. There were many things uncertain, but Dawlish couldn't mistake Kate's delight at Calder's presence. Nor could he Martson's. Both were completely on top of the world.

Why?

It couldn't be because of the *Royal Commission* report; it could hardly be to do with the store of toys. There was an unknown factor—the 'something else' which worried Trivett, although he'd never got round to saying what it was, or even giving a hint.

Then Calder said: 'All right.' He wiped his forehead. 'All right. But if I join you again, Martson, I want to know everything about the distribution. Everything.'

CHAPTER XXV

MARTSON'S DELIGHT

A glow of delight gleamed in Martson's faded eyes and seemed to pour new life into him. Kate sat down, as if it were almost too much for her.

'Yes, yes, of course, we shall be equal partners,' said Martson.

Calder said: 'I'll want safeguards.'

'You shall have them. And we shall have to have safeguards, too. We can go into all that later, can't we? Let us consider the mutual advantages of working together. I have a world-wide sales organisation, not to mention quite a strong body of men in England who will do whatever I tell them, because I pay them well, and because—well, they would rather be safe and work with me than go against me and find themselves in prison. So, I've the sales organisation which is foolproof, and of course I've the drugs. Don't underestimate the importance of the drugs, will you?'

'I don't,' said Calder.

Now that he'd reached a decision, confidence seemed to ooze back into him. Had Calder really been so frightened? Or had he bluffed? Dawlish remembered the way he'd wiped his forehead, as if he were wringing with sweat—and yet his forehead hadn't been at all shiny. He looked fantastically handsome. Kate was just beyond him; they made a fine pair.

Calder said: 'I don't know how you got Dawlish to work with you, but I wouldn't trust him an inch. I'm not talking about anything while Dawlish is here.'

'Dawlish is *quite* reliable,' said Martson softly.

'He's done wonders,' said Kate, but didn't look at Dawlish. 'I just don't know how we would have got on without him. If he hadn't taken the keys from Mick Ryan, the police would have found them, and then they'd have been brought back to you. Think what a disappointment it would have been for us!'

'I'm not going to talk in front of Dawlish,' said Calder very deliberately. 'You must have some hold over him, or he wouldn't work for you, but he's not sharing my secrets. Send him out of the room.'

Silence fell upon them all. Kate and Martson looked as if they felt awkward and uncomfortable. Calder, fully composed again, stretched out his legs and adjusted his trousers neatly.

'We can decide what to do about him later. If you take my advice, you'll put him where he can't talk,' said Calder. 'Get out, Dawlish.'

Dawlish stayed where he was.

Kate flashed a glance at him; pleading, even beseeching: 'Look,' the glance said, 'we've got practically everything, we just want one more thing, and we can get it if you'll be a good boy and go outside.' Martson looked down at the desk, furtively. But none of this was really genuine; it was more play-acting, for his benefit.

Martson didn't lift his eyes.

'Dawlish, I'm sure you understand—'

'Pat,' murmured Kate.

Dawlish said: 'I'm with you on a fifty-fifty basis, and that means a half-share of everything, including information. I'm staying here.'

Martson's voice became more mincing than ever. 'Dawlish, I don't want to be unfair, but there are some things which we have to keep to ourselves. If you wouldn't mind waiting outside for a few minutes, we'd all be grateful. Don't spoil the good work you've already done.'

Kate came to his side, and took his arm.

'Come with me, Pat,' she said, and whispered: 'Don't be a fool.' Neither of the others could have heard that whisper, and neither could actually see her lips.

'Dawlish, don't make me use violent methods,' said Martson. His hand hovered over the desk—above a bell-push. 'I don't want to bring the others in just now. Be a good fellow. It's only a matter of time.'

'Pat—' whispered Kate.

She tugged at his arm, and he moved slowly towards the door. He was more than ever certain that Trivett was right; there was something much bigger than drugs behind all this. Kate held on to his arm, and unlocked the door and went outside with him. She pushed the door to; the key turned in the lock; so Martson had followed them. She didn't speak again, but pressed his arm gently and led the way along a passage to another room—a bedroom. It wasn't well furnished, was a poor setting for her, but she looked radiant.

'If you're double-crossing me—' Dawlish began.

'Don't be silly, darling. This is exactly what we want. Calder will go into details with Martson. Marston will tell me, then you and I will be able to deal with Martson and negotiate with Calder ourselves. He won't really care who he's dealing with, provided he knows he's safe. Sit down, Pat.'

He sat in a large arm-chair.

She sat on the arm and rested her arm on his shoulders.

'It must have been a strain, but it's nearly over. You've had a rough time—you haven't really recovered from the accident. When I think that they nearly killed you, I could—' she broke off, and gave a little, low-pitched laugh. 'But they didn't. It doesn't matter.'

Her arm slid round his neck.

'When I look into the future, Pat, I can hardly believe what I see.'

'Can't you?' asked Dawlish. Must he trust her? Hope that she meant what she said, and would pass on all that Martson told her? Could he trust her, even if she really believed in his 'conversion'? She was soft and yielding, a vision and a dream—and yet he knew he couldn't trust her. She was playing a part, just as Calder had been. Calder suave, self-possessed; Calder nervous; Calder frightened; Calder refusing to do a deal with Martson, then suddenly giving way; Calder recovering his pose, getting cocky, ordering Dawlish out. It was all part of an act, like wiping his forehead.

Kate was acting, too.

Martson wasn't, and Steen hadn't been. There hadn't been any mistake about the glow of delight in Martson's eyes when Calder had said he would agree. Now they were in a huddle in the next room; exchanging—what? The information that Trivett wanted, and to which he'd gone to such lengths to get.

'Why don't you have a nap?' asked Kate. 'Or would you rather have a drink?' She put her cheek against his. 'Pat, be careful what you do in the next few hours. Don't let them suspect that you and I are plotting against them.'

She *was* play-acting; just like Calder.

Remember that Calder was handsome as a Greek god, and Kate a fitting mate for him—and that they'd once lived together.

Kate and Calder.

'What is it?' she asked, for she felt him stiffen and shift himself so that he was more upright.

'Nothing. I don't trust those two together, my sweet.' He stood up, with her clinging to him. 'It's time I went to investigate.'

'Let me go and see how they're getting on,' she said. 'I'll tell them you're losing patience. Try not to force anything now.'

He looked undecided.

'I'll be back in a few minutes,' she promised, and slipped out of the room. She closed the door softly behind her.

There was no other sound—until something fell, outside—a chair or a table, which thudded and then clattered. Someone swore, and Kate said: 'Are you hurt?' Dawlish didn't hear the answer.

He went to the door and turned the handle.

The door was locked.

She'd locked it, under the cover of that falling object—so that he wouldn't hear the key turn. Cunning Kate! should he wait, and pretend that he didn't know what had happened? He lit a cigarette and waited; seconds seemed like minutes. The curious thing was that after the crash and the voices, he'd heard nothing. Suddenly he did hear something; a creak, then stealthy movements, as if someone were creeping towards his door. Perhaps she was coming to unlock it. He sat on the arm of the chair, waiting for the handle to turn. It didn't. The stealthy movements outside continued—then faded. He thought he heard a door close, and knew he heard a car start up and move along the road.

He went to the window. It overlooked back gardens and some houses opposite.

He went to the door again; it was still locked. He took out his penknife, and selected a blade which could be used as a skeleton key. He started to work on the lock. It wasn't hard to pick—a simple door lock. He hesitated before it sprang back; and the little click sounded very loud.

He opened the door.

The light was still on the landing.

He saw no one as he moved towards the room where he had left Martson and Calder. He fancied that he smelt perfume; *Lida*. He tried the handle of the door, and it wasn't locked, but the room was in darkness. Panic, the panic which follows utter defeat, seized him; and he didn't thrust the door open, but pushed it gently. It creaked; had that been the sound he had heard before the stealthy movements started? He had the door open wide enough to get through, now, and groped for the light switch.

He pressed it down.

Light flooded the room, and shone on Martson, who lay sprawled on the desk, with his head battered to pulp.

Everything had been taken from the desk.

The house was empty. Except for the room where he had been with Kate, it had an unlived-in atmosphere. Beds were made, drawers were empty. In the narrow kitchen there were several recently opened tins and some dirty crockery, but that was all. In the room next to the kitchen was a camp bed, unmade that day. There was a photograph of Mulligan in sailor's uniform— and he remembered advising the Haslemere police to look for an old salt if they wanted to find who had flogged Mick Ryan with the cat.

He went back to the main room, and his lips tightened when he saw Martson, whom he hadn't touched. The man's face lay in his own blood. The blood hadn't splashed far; it was mostly on the desk.

The telephone rang.

He snatched it up.

'Get away from there,' a man said. 'The police are coming.'

CHAPTER XXVI

WANTED

The voice wasn't familiar; its owner didn't say any more, but hung up. The ringing tone and the words echoed in Dawlish's ears as he tried to understand why he had been warned, and who had warned him. Did that matter? He could see the trick, now; the depth of its cunning oughtn't to surprise him, and yet—it did.

Kate and Calder, both acting a part—of course they were working together. They'd killed Martson and gone off, and the police were on the way. Kate and Calder had been after Martson's secret, not Kate and Martson after Calder's. As far as Kate and Calder were concerned, the police wanted Dawlish.

Who had warned him to leave?

Should he leave or stay? There was no real danger for him as the police knew what he was doing, but—he hadn't finished the job. A few minutes before he had felt that surge of panic, springing from the fear of complete failure, but—he wasn't prepared to give in, yet. Calder had that something, and he had to find it and find out what it was.

He hurried from the room.

No one was in the street. The car had gone. He turned left, away from the shop at the corner, and passed Kate's garage. The doors were open. A car engine sounded, and he saw the glow of headlights as they spread from the far end of the street, reaching him. He turned the corner. The light grew brighter, but he thought that the car stopped. Yes, the engine was switched off. He hurried across the road and down a narrow valley. Another car swept along the road he had just left; no doubt the police had approached from each side. He hurried on, reached some rows of mean little houses, and saw the huge skeleton of a ware-house just ahead of him. A tug hooted mournfully on the river, like a wailing siren warning of a raid. He reached another main road and hurried along it until at last he saw a red two-decker bus. He was safe enough from the police.

Safe!

He laughed, for the first time since he had seen Martson's head. A drizzle of rain began to fall, and he turned up his coat collar. He stopped in the main road until the bus came up. He went upstairs; only half a dozen people were there, including a couple in a huddle on the back seat. The girl giggled as he glanced round at them.

The conductor came up.

'Fares pliz.'

'How far do you go?'

'Aldgit.'

'All the way,' said Dawlish. He didn't think he had been followed from Killiger Street, but he looked round once or twice, to see whether any car was following close upon the bus. There was none. Two cyclists dropped behind. The girl on the back seat giggled again. Dawlish lit a cigarette, and peered at the rain which now speckled the glass.

He felt as if he were on the run; the worst of the play-acting had yet to come. There was no need for him to be afraid of the police, and yet—if he were still to find out the truth, Kate and Calder would have to believe that he was.

The bus stopped and he saw the lights of an underground station.

'Aldgit, all change!' called the conductor.

Dawlish went downstairs and passed two human derelicts leaning against the pillar of the station. He saw a policeman talking to a ticket inspector at the barrier. The man looked at him speculatively—almost accusingly. No, that was imagination; it couldn't be anything else.

It was raining.

If he were really on the run, where would he go?

To Felicity? No, the police would be watching.

To Tim's flat, or Beresford's; or to the club; No, the police would be watching all of those. To a small hotel? There didn't seem much choice. Of course, he could go to Milton Square and demand sanctuary from Calder, but—that wouldn't serve, just yet!

Then the notion came to him. He snapped his fingers, making two passers-by stare. He grinned broadly. Of course, the very place to hide—Bert's garage. It wasn't very far from here, within walking distance. Bert was a character, and Bert could be trusted.

Bert was cleaning down his cab and whistling. He owned three cabs, one of which he drove himself, and this was the only one in the garage. He didn't look round as Dawlish came in, but said:

'Sorry, guv'. Can't go out again to-night.'

'Not even for me?' asked Dawlish.

Bert swung round. 'Strewth! I didn't expect to see *you*, Guv'nor.' He tossed a wash-leather on to a box and wiped his hands on the seat of his trousers. ''Arf a mo', I'll get me coat,' he said. 'Where we going?'

'I don't know,' said Dawlish.

'Moon do you okay?'

'Bert, I'm serious,' said Dawlish. 'I want to hide out for a day or two.'

'*Do* yer,' breathed Bert. 'Who from?'

'The police.'

'*You!*' Bert couldn't have said more plainly that he didn't believe it.

'I'm still serious,' said Dawlish. 'Things have gone wrong. There'll be a hunt for me. I want to stay somewhere for a day or two, until—'

'If you go on like this, Mr. Dawlish, I'll believe yer,' said Bert, wiping his hands on the seat of his trousers again.

'I want you to. I'm in a spot.'

'Oh,' said Bert slowly. He took out a cigarette-making machine and some tobacco. 'Well, that takes some beating. But—sure, I'll give you cover, Mr. Dawlish. I—'

'Quickly?'

'Yeh. Now. Upstairs. I live upstairs,' said Bert. 'I'll square it wiv the missus—often told 'er abaht yer, I 'ave. Come on, now, 'urry if you're in a n'urry.'

The feeling that he was in an unfamiliar place came to him when he woke up and before he opened his eyes. It was broad daylight. He lay for a few minutes, collecting his thoughts, remembering where he was.

Bert tapped at the door, and came in with a cup of tea, some newspapers and a long face. His wife was in the room behind him, and took a peek at Dawlish over Bert's shoulder as he shut the door with great ostentation. He put the tea on a bamboo bedside table and dropped the papers on to the bed. Then he stood back as if asking for an explanation.

Dawlish's photograph was on the front page of each of the three newspapers; so was the word '*Wanted*'. Dawlish scanned the first story. There wasn't really much in it. Patrick Dawlish was wanted by the police in connection with the death of William Steen and Jacob Martson; it was also believed that the police were anxious to interview him in connection with the body found in Burn Street. There followed a brief but sensational account of Dawlish's past, beginning from the time when he had been on the staff of M.I.5.

It was the *Daily Crier* which really got under Dawlish's skin. The tabloid had a photograph of Felicity, and reported that a special correspondent had interviewed Mrs. Dawlish, but she could give no information about her husband's movements.

Side by side with the picture of Felicity he seemed to see the photograph of Helen and himself.

He forgot Bert, until Bert coughed.

'Oh, hallo,' said Dawlish. 'Not good, Bert, is it?'

'What 'ave you bin up to, Mr. Dawlish?' Bert sounded dispirited. 'I don't want any trouble.'

'Is anyone hanging about outside?'

'Yes, there is, and my missus don't like it,' said Bert. 'Look out the window!'

Dawlish, wearing singlet and trunks, stepped across the room. Through the mesh of the lace curtains he saw a man lounging near a small café on the opposite side of the road.

It was Ken.

So Kate hadn't killed him.

'I don't like saying it, Mr. Dawlish, but you can see you can't stay arahnd 'ere, can't yer?' Bert shuffled his feet. 'Maybe I could fix something. I got a pal who runs a doss-house. Not much of a place, but 'e's got some privit rooms. If you need some cash, Mr. Dawlish, I could manage twenty quid.'

'No money, Bert, thanks, but for the rest—thanks.'

He went back into his room. 'I'd like to use the telephone before I go.'

The telephone was in a small office in a corner of the garage. Dawlish closed the door, and had hardly room to move. He dialled Scotland Yard, and was annoyed because his heart began to pump vigorously. The calm official voice of the operator did little to steady it. He asked for Trivett, and held on; he wouldn't give his name.

'Bill, know who this is?'

'Thank the Lord you've come through,' said Trivett. He lowered his voice. 'No names. Are you all right? I was afraid they'd fixed you, although I heard you'd answered the 'phone when we tipped you off about the raid.'

'Why raid at all just then?'

'Calder gave us a tip. If we hadn't taken it, he'd have known it was a frame-up. He named you. Are you all right?'

'More or less. Shadowed. I haven't got much farther, except that Calder and Kate are working together, and always have been. They've been after something Martson could give them, and Martson after something they had. Two halves of the same thing, I gather. I don't know yet what it is.'

'I do,' said Trivett, breaking his long pretence.

'Well, what is it?'

'Sorry. Top secret, even now. It's got a lot of important people badly worried. We knew Calder had part of this thing, suspected someone had the other—we didn't know it was Martson. Now the two pieces are together, and it's dynamite.'

'What's to stop you from raiding Calder's house and getting it all?' asked Dawlish.

'The danger that Calder will destroy records which matter more than the thing itself,' said Trivett. 'Have you still a chance of getting in with them?'

Dawlish said slowly: 'I can try.'

'Try,' said Trivett. 'We'll leave it to you—we'll watch you and help if we can, but you're really on your own. If you fail, we'll have to make the best of it and raid Calder's place, but—much better if you can fix it all.'

'All right,' said Dawlish. 'If there's any message, send it to Mr. Denton, *post restante*, Aldgate Post Office.'

There wasn't any way he could avoid going on. He could resent the fact that it was still top secret, but Trivett wouldn't have gone to these lengths unless he were acting under orders from someone high up. Top secret, and the way it was being handled, meant Government secret. No, there was nothing to do but go on.

The 'privit' room at the doss house was a box of a place with a tiny window. It smelt; the whole house smelt, of dirt and decay and unwashed human flesh. On the ground floor was a big room, the common room, where tramps and small-time crooks and others on the road or on the run jostled over the one small gas-ring, to cook their food. On the next floor was a huge dormitory. On the next, the private rooms. Dawlish paid ten pounds in advance; was brought some food which revolted him—was also brought the papers. The scream for him grew louder. Felicity's photograph appeared in most of the papers too. There was no mention of Tim, but several references to the Burn Street 'body.'

All the time, Ken, Mobey, or another man kept watch on the doss house.

They'd let him come here, from the garage.

Would they let him reach Milton Square?

On the afternoon of the second day, he sent a messenger to the post office, for any letters for 'Mr. Denton.' There was none; so Calder was still in residence, therefore still confident. The hunt for Dawlish must be reassuring for him, but—wouldn't he feel safer with Dawlish dead?

After dark on the second evening, Dawlish went out, his coat collar turned up, an old peaked cap pulled over his eyes. He saw and recognised Ken. He hunched his shoulders and walked along the street towards Mile End Road. Ken followed. The gloom was brightened only by glows from a few lamps which made an area of brightness at intervals. Each time Dawlish passed beneath one he felt his muscles tensing. Afraid—lest a bullet or a knife should come out of the dark. Lest a car should swing round a corner, and get him, this time. These dark stretches of the mean streets brought something near terror.

Hunched shoulders, and the peaked cap prevented him from being noticeable when he reached a bus stop and joined a small queue.

Ken also joined it.

CHAPTER XXVII

TOP SECRET

The bus was a Number 15.

Dawlish alighted half-way along Oxford Street; so did Ken. The bright lights and the throngs of people seemed strange after the two days of enforced loneliness. Dawlish slipped into a side street and, still shuffling and keeping his knees bent, to disguise his height, walked towards Milton Square. It would take him twenty minutes.

Ken followed.

Again Dawlish felt the gathering threat of panic when he was in dark stretches of the streets. Panic, because of the possibility of failure and the importance of success. Failure would be ready made if Ken had instructions to prevent him from reaching Calder's house.

The walk seemed never-ending, but he reached the square at last, passed the doorway in which Tim had hidden when he had first raided the place. He crossed the road; Ken followed. He glanced up and down as he approached Calder's house, and, seeing only Ken, darted up the steps and on to the porch. His finger hovered over the bell-push.

'Ring three times,' said Ken.

Dawlish whirled round—as if he hadn't known the man was anywhere near. Ken grinned.

'Didn't know I was around, did you, Dawlish? You've made a lot of mistakes. Ring three times.'

Dawlish drew away from the bell.

'Okay, *I'll* ring,' said Ken. He pushed forward and stabbed the bell-push viciously. Then they waited, while two cars passed along the street. In the gloom, Dawlish could see Ken's face and his satisfied grin.

One of the big huskies opened the door.

'Okay,' said Ken. 'Take him straight up, Winkie.'

Ken didn't come in; his duty, obviously, was to stay on guard outside. The husky dropped his right hand to his pocket and Dawlish needed no telling that he held a gun.

Dawlish walked up the stairs, sensing again the quietness which had brooded over this house when he had first come to see Calder. The husky reached the door of the library just in front of him, gripped his arm, and then tapped on the door; four times.

A key grated in the lock, and the door was opened by Kate.

'Pat, *darling*,' cooed Kate.

'I hoped you'd come,' said Calder.

'But,' went on Calder, 'don't get any fool notion that you can do any damage, Dawlish.' He went to the graceful desk and sat down, took out a snub-nosed automatic from his pocket, and laid it on the desk. 'Sit down.'

Dawlish took a chair opposite the desk. The light glinted on a cut-glass decanter full of what looked like whisky.

'You haven't shaved,' murmured Kate.

She looked more beautiful than ever. Something had brushed her eyes and her cheeks with radiance. Yes, she was loveliness itself—and she matched Calder's handsomeness perfectly. Dawlish looked from one to the other, sensing that beneath their smiles there was tension. Compared with Calder's immaculate grooming, he was like a tramp; and doubtless the smell of the doss-house hung about him.

'Why have you come, Pat?' asked Kate.

'I want to get out of the country.'

'Yes, the police are making it hot for you,' said Calder. 'After all, three murders is going the pace. Steen—Jeremy—Martson. Even the great Dawlish should know where to stop.'

Dawlish said: 'Are you going to get me out of the country? I can't go to my bank, can't get my hands on any cash. I can't get out on my passport, either, I need a fake one. And tickets—a shipping berth. Or I could work my way to South America, if it came to that, but—why the hell should I work when you're sitting pretty here.'

'He sings a different tune to-night,' said Calder. 'Yes, we'll get you out of the country, Dawlish.'

'What's the catch?'

'You'll have to work your passage, but it won't make you sweat. If you ever slip up, Dawlish, you'll be extradited, brought back here and—hanged. You know that, don't you? We've witnesses. We've already sent two of them to report to the police, that's why the hunt's so strong. If you fail us, you'll be finished. Got that? All right. You know a bit about our organisation, don't you, Dawlish? We want messages taken to some of our agents abroad. About fresh supplies of the drugs. And we want them to know that Kate's taken charge in place of Martson. *You'll* take the messages. You'll go by air, in a private aircraft.'

'Why use me? Why don't you use someone else?'

Kate laughed. 'There aren't many people we would trust, are there, Jeremiah?'

'That doesn't fool me,' said Dawlish. 'Why use me?' He didn't know; it didn't make sense that they'd use him for such a mission as this, unless—he'd worked better than he knew, hoodwinked them completely. Success loomed nearer, and yet—would they deliver precious secrets to him?

'You don't ask questions, you just do what you're told,' said Calder. 'Will you play?'

'I haven't any choice.'

'It's a good thing you realise that,' said Calder, and laughed again, explosively. 'I can't think of anyone I'd rather use, Dawlish. You'll have some papers with you and will deliver copies to each of the agents I'm going to name. You'll finish up in South America where I've a big agency. You'll be able to live and work there. Look after me, and I'll look after you.'

Dawlish said: 'I still don't know why you've picked on me.'

'Don't you, darling?' asked Kate. 'It's because we think you've got the guts to get through.'

He licked his lips and looked at the decanter meaningly, but Calder pretended not to notice the stare. 'You've been working with Calder all the time, haven't you?'

'All the time,' agreed Kate lightly. 'I've never really left Jeremiah, but Martson got half of what we needed, so I had to go and work with him. But he wanted the other half, which Jeremiah had. He thought I could break into the strong room—but I couldn't. I knew young Mick Ryan well, though, and put Martson on to Mick. Jeremiah let Mick have the keys. He thought the best way to get both parts of the thing we wanted was to let Martson have them first. Then—we took them away. I worked with them both and with you, *darling*. But I'd bought Ken and Mobey and everyone else, except Steen—Steen was loyal to Martson. That's why I was so glad when you killed him. Then I wanted you to trust me, so I had that attack made on me. Poor darling, you behaved so well. Quite the gallant.'

Dawlish licked his lips again.

'Without you, Martson would never have got the other part—the vital second part—of that document. Without you, Jeremiah couldn't have made a visit to Martson, and made him give him all the details of the organisation for distributing the drugs. That's important, you see—the drug agents will act for us in the other thing.'

Calder snapped: 'Kate!'

'Other thing?' asked Dawlish gratingly.

'Just another little business we run on the side,' said Kate, but she looked vexed with herself.

Dawlish said heavily: 'Before I do anything, I'm going to know what it's all about.'

'You're mistaken,' said Calder. He grinned. 'It's a top secret. You just carry out your orders from now on, Dawlish. Don't forget if you make a slip, you'll be hauled back to England and you'll be hanged.'

Kate said: 'We're in complete control, Pat. You just have to do what you're told. Everything about the top secret is in this room, and—'

'Kate!' Calder snapped again.

'Well, isn't it?' asked Kate. She dropped her hand from her chin, and her fingers touched the barrel of Calder's gun. Even Dawlish had no idea what she was going to do—until she pulled the gun towards her, as if she were playing with it, and then suddenly took it by the handle.

She covered Calder.

'Yes, Pat,' she said. 'Everything's here, in this room. Don't move, Jeremiah. Everything, Pat—the top secret. The agents' names and addresses, here and abroad. All the details, everything you want. Shall we have the keys?'

She smiled at Calder.

Calder rose from his chair, then sank back again, looked from Kate to Dawlish and back again. He didn't speak. Dawlish recovered from the spasm of incredulous astonishment, and stood up. He reached forward and moved the decanter out of Calder's reach. He didn't yet understand, but—Kate *had* always insisted she was 'for him.'

He said: 'Nice work, Kate.' He took the gun from her.

Calder made a queer noise in his throat.

'I thought you'd think so, Pat,' said Kate. How superbly beautiful she was! 'I couldn't do much until both halves of the puzzle were placed together. I had to let Calder kill Martson, so that it could be done. They're together in this room. Even here, I couldn't get them out on my own. Jeremiah has always been suspicious of everyone; he's never fully trusted me. If I'd taken the keys from him, alone—anything might have happened. I can do what I like now with Ken and the outside men, but not with the bodyguard indoors. They belong to Jeremiah. Think you can get past them, Pat?'

'Try me!'

'You've—double-crossed me,' Calder said. It wasn't said harshly or bitterly, but sounded like a sigh—as if he wouldn't believe what he had heard.

'But yes, Jeremiah. How I've worked, double-crossing everyone, just making sure those two halves got together. You see, Pat, Jeremiah got the whole thing. Martson stole half of it. Both halves are vital.'

'You—you and Dawlish—' Calder still sighed.

'Such good friends, aren't we?' cooed Kate. 'Actually, Pat didn't know, but we work for the same boss—His Majesty's

Government. Trivett didn't let on, Pat, did he? It's been done so delicately, from the beginning. After all, it's a delicate matter. I can tell you now, Pat. That *Royal Commission Report* was a dummy. There were two reports on it—one in invisible ink. Details of the disposition of our armed forces. Details of new inventions. Statements about atomic energy, the latest in rockets, the latest in jet-propulsion. The secret report was in two parts. Martson got one, because he was so anxious to find out what the *Commission* knew about drugs. He tested the paper and found the other information, but half of it was no use to him.

'And Calder, who'd stolen the report—as I told you—had the other half.

'I'd been working on Calder for a long time, because he wasn't trusted. What sacrifices I made in the course of duty, Jeremiah!'

CHAPTER XXVIII

TOP DRAWER

Calder spoke in that sighing, bewildered voice.

'So you're a spy, Kate. I let you fool me.'

'It wasn't so very hard,' said Kate.

'I should have known, when you were so anxious to have Dawlish with us. I should have known Dawlish was working with the police.'

Dawlish understood now. Everything.

'You should have known a lot of things,' he said.

'I knew just a few,' said Calder. He smoothed down his hair. 'I knew that the time might come when I'd have to drop everything. I've had a good run.'

'And it's over.'

'Yes. You'll come with me,' said Calder. He smiled, as if he hadn't a worry in the world. 'Both of you. I've always played high, Kate. You know that. The richest man in the world—and I would have been had I sold these secrets. The dream's gone up into thin air, as we shall. A wise man always makes sure of his retreat. I knew I might lose. I knew I couldn't face a trial. So, I protected myself from that. Fixed to my chair is a little switch;

fixed to the switch, a wire; fixed to the wire, high explosive, which will blow this room into thin air. I wouldn't be surprised if it blows quite a hole in the roof, too. I wonder if we'll meet in the other place, Kate.'

'Oh, no,' said Kate. 'I thought the wire was to call for help if you ever had trouble in here. I cut it this afternoon. I—Pat!'

Calder leapt from his chair, snatching at his coat; at a gun. It flashed out and he fired at her as Dawlish fired at his wrist. Kate gave a little soughing sound, half-rose, then dropped again. Blood oozed up on her temple as she slumped back in her chair.

Blood dripped from Calder's wrist.

Dawlish didn't shoot again, but hit him savagely. Calder rocked back on his heels while the echo of the shot still sounded in the room. Dawlish let him fall and seized the telephone. It was connected with the exchange. He dialled WHI 1212. Footsteps thumped outside, someone began to batter on the door. The Yard operator answered. 'Tell Trivett. Calder's house. Urgent.' Dawlish replaced the receiver, curiously calm as the thudding grew louder on the door, and the walls shook. He got up, pushed a heavy chair beneath the handle of the door, then went back and sat at Kate's side. He held his gun in his hand. The chair shivered and the door began to give. He wondered idly whether Trivett could get men here in time. If not—no doubt that they'd kill him, being loyal to Calder. It didn't greatly matter: Kate had paid one price, he could pay another, different one. True, she might have to pay twice, perhaps she had already. First as Calder's mistress; then with her life. Incredible! He'd not got within miles of the truth, and yet—it was all so simple although it had seemed so complicated.

The door was shaking violently.

He heard men talking in whispers outside.

'If anyone shows his nose, I'll shoot it off,' said Dawlish.

There were other sounds, from downstairs, yet they were very like the nearer ones: heavy thudding. The man who had called out, snapped: 'What's that?'

'Only the police,' said Dawlish loudly. 'Pop down and let them in, will you?'

There was quiet on the landing; and a crash downstairs.

The police caught all of the huskies as they tried to get out the back way. They caught Mobey and Ken; and, later, Ken's men. They found everything they wanted in a safe built into the floor of Calder's room.

Felicity was in London—at Ted Beresford's flat. Tim was also there, according to Trivett. Felicity had heard that Tim was hurt, and had hurried up to town. Naturally. She would have done in any circumstances, and yet Dawlish wished she hadn't. Vast dangers had been avoided, thanks to Kate. Kate, who'd been prepared to give anything, and even to kill Tim, in order to get what she desperately needed.

Kate was in St. Thomas's Hospital. Not dead, not even likely to die. They'd operated and saved her life.

He hadn't shaved, he was a disreputable-looking hulk of a man as he stepped out of a taxi at Beresford's flat in Chelsea. There were lights at the front window of the flat, which was on the second floor. He went slowly upstairs. Trivett hadn't telephoned Felicity yet, Dawlish hadn't wanted him to. Felicity had brought Helen up, Helen had gone to stay with friends.

He reached the front door, and his fingers touched the bell-push. He pressed it sharply.

The huge form of Ted Beresford appeared in the doorway. His ugly, homely face was transformed as he saw who it was.

'Good lord,' said Beresford. 'I didn't think—'

A door behind him opened, and Felicity came into the hall. Her face was pale and her eyes were shadowed. she said: 'Ted, leave us, please.' The door closed: Dawlish and Felicity were together.

She put out a hand.

'Pat, I can't—think what's happened. But you shouldn't have come here and—risked trouble for Ted. God knows what devil's got into you, but it's not Ted's problem, not Tim's either. I'll get my hat and coat.'

'To go where?' asked Dawlish.

'I—I don't know. I've got plenty of money. Tim and Ted have helped me to get a false passport for you. And for me, of course. But, Pat, please don't stay here.'

'What happens, if we're caught together?'

Felicity said: 'Worry about that if it happens. You—you're not yourself; I may be able to help.'

'Oh, my darling,' said Dawlish, and his voice was unsteady. She looked at him with swimming eyes, then suddenly lurched forward, and his arms enfolded her.

'Pat, what's happened to you? I can't—I can't understand it. Oh, it—it doesn't matter.' She strained against him. 'We must hurry, we mustn't stay here, the—the flat was watched all the afternoon. Let me go, Pat. Hurry.'

He didn't.

'*Tim* helped with passports?' he asked.

'Yes. He—they—they know you can't be yourself. If we can get away, somewhere quiet—'

'What it is to have friends,' said Dawlish, and his voice was husky. 'Fel, look at me.' The grey-green of her eyes was brilliant with tears and—something deeper. 'It's all been fake, Fel. Trivett will be here soon, just to confirm. *All* faked—as phoney as that photograph of me and Helen.'

She was rigid in his arms.

'Tim!' called Dawlish. 'Ted!'

The door opened; they must have been standing close to it. Both men were framed against the light of the room beyond.

'Just wanted to say thanks,' said Dawlish gruffly. 'And then to call you a pair of mutton-heads. Trivett will be here soon. He'll tell you that I tipped him off to come and get you ready for the stomach pump, Tim. He'll tell you a lot of other things. It's over. Calder the chief villain.'

Tim said: 'What?' rather vaguely. 'Er—*Kate*?'

'Perhaps Trivett can tell you all about her too. I can't. Only that she's out of the top drawer.'

They saw Kate in hospital next morning. Her head was bandaged, but it didn't dim the lustre of her eyes. They lit up as Dawlish and Felicity entered the small ward. Little was said, but Dawlish had to ask one question: about Tim and the arsenic.

Kate smiled.

'I saw you hurrying up the street and guessed what you were doing. But I had to pretend that I didn't. There wasn't any arsenic in that whisky, Pat. Only face powder.'

ABOUT THE AUTHOR

John Creasey, born in 1908, was a paramount English crime and science fiction writer who used myriad pseudonyms for more than six hundred novels. He founded the UK Crime Writers' Association in 1953. In 1962, his book *Gideon's Fire* received the Edgar Award for Best Novel from the Mystery Writers of America. Many of the characters featured in Creasey's titles became popular, including George Gideon of Scotland Yard, who was the basis for a subsequent television series and film. Creasey died in Salisbury, UK, in 1973.

THE PATRICK DAWLISH MYSTERIES

FROM OPEN ROAD MEDIA

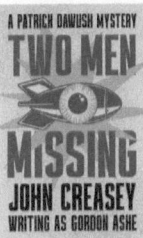  

OPEN ROAD

INTEGRATED MEDIA

OPEN ROAD

INTEGRATED MEDIA

Find a full list of our authors and
titles at www.openroadmedia.com

FOLLOW US
@OpenRoadMedia